Praise for
THE UNREMEMBERED
and
Trial of Intentions
Books One & Two of
The Vault of Heaven

"Engaging characters and powerful storytelling in the tradition of Robert Jordan, Terry Goodkind, and Dennis L. McKiernan make this a top-notch fantasy by a new author to watch."
— *Library Journal* (Starred review)

"A sprawling, complex tale of magic and destiny that won't disappoint its readers. This auspicious beginning for author Peter Orullian will have you looking forward to more." — Terry Brooks

"The Vault of Heaven is an ambitious story in the mold of Robert Jordan and Terry Goodkind. Peter Orullian is a name to watch in the field of epic fantasy." — Kevin J. Anderson

"This is one huge, powerful, compelling, hard-hitting story . . . The Vault of Heaven is a major fantasy adventure." — Piers Anthony

"A fine debut!" — Brandon Sanderson

"Great fantasy tales plunge us into vivid new worlds, in the company of fascinating characters. The Vault of Heaven is great fantasy. It grips you and shows you true friendship, strange places, and heroes growing to confront world-shaking evil. Magnificent! I want more!"
— Ed Greenwood

"The Vault of Heaven by Peter Orullian is a vast canvas filled with thought-provoking ideas on the questions of good and evil that engage us all." — Anne Perry

"Intricately crafted with its own distinct melody, *The Unremembered* is a groundbreaking work of epic fantasy." ∼ Bookwormblues.net

"Sometimes you just need a big, fat fantasy, and Peter Orullian's re-mastered edition of *The Unremembered* delivers everything you're looking for: a fascinating world, tense action, charismatic characters, and a magic system the like of which you've never imagined."

∼ Aidan Moher
A Dribble of Ink
Hugo Award Winner

"*The Unremembered* captures the unique essence and mystery of music, and weaves it into every line of a compelling and exciting world, while telling a character-driven story that resonates through the ages . . . a work of art on par with the masters of the genre, Jordan, Rothfuss, Tolkien, and more."

∼ Elitistbookreviews.com
2013 & 2014 Hugo-nominated
for best review site

"Engaging characters, complex magic, and expertly written—a whole new kind of epic fantasy!" ∼ Suvudu.com

"Orullian's *Trial of Intentions* is a tale of music and magic, of daring and sacrifice, in an intricate and believable world." ∼ Robin Hobb

"Peter Orullian's *Trial of Intentions* is a book enormous in scope and in intricacy, with a welter of political, cultural, and magical intrigues, behind which lies the role of song in preserving a myriad of cultures, all of which disagree with each other to some extent, even as it becomes apparent to the reader that, without some degree of cooperation, all will suffer, if not perish. A challenging story about challenged cultures, and one well-told."

∼ L. E. Modesitt, Jr.

THE VAULT OF HEAVEN

STORY VOLUME ONE

PETER ORULLIAN

descantpublishing

This one's for Roland Deschain
and
For all of you still using the phrase,
"The hell you say!"

Also by Peter Orullian

The Unremembered
Trial of Intentions

TABLE OF CONTENTS

Foreword   i

Battle of the Round   1

With What's Familiar   35

Sacrifice of the First Sheason   69

Civil War 119

A Blade of Grass 135

The Great Defense of Layosah 165

Preview: Author's Edition of *The Unremembered* 201

About Peter Orullian 235

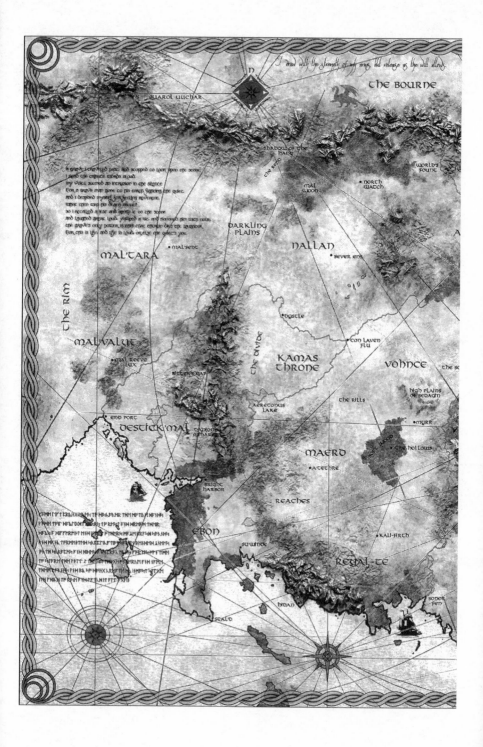

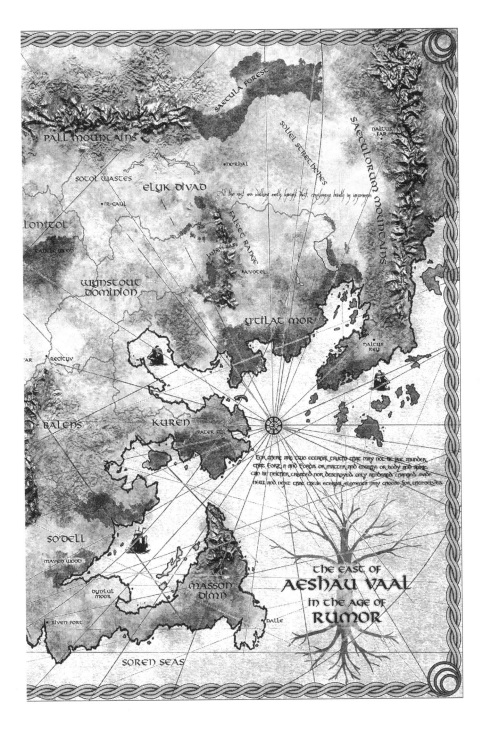

THE EAST OF
AESHAU VAAL
IN THE AGE OF
RUMOR

FOREWORD

VEN IN A BIG fat fantasy, you leave things out. There's just not
room for all the world building. Otherwise, it would read like
a history. So, often times—for me anyway—entire events get a
passing nod in a novel. They add authentic detail. But the truth is
there's a story behind each tidbit.

And some of these stories want to be told.

That's what this volume is: a collection of stories set in the world
of my epic fantasy series, The Vault of Heaven. The tales here have
all been written to stand on their own. So, if you haven't read my
novels, never fear.

That said, there's also a nice resonance that occurs when you
read both the short stories and the novels. If you read the short
stories first, then when you happen upon a reference to them in
the books, you'll have a satisfying "aha" moment, since you'll understand the deeper context. If you've read the books first, then
coming to the stories can be an interesting side-journey to explore
an event that's only been hinted at in the books.

All of which is to say, it's not necessary to read both. Just more
fun, I think. And for my part, some of these stories I waited ten

years to write. I knew I'd write them eventually. Some, I even dreaded writing—I'll talk more about that in the story intros.

Some of the characters you'll read about are part of the long past in the world I've created. Some you'll see in the current timeline of the series. And taken together, they help weave an overarching fabric with the novels to tell a story about a world, its people, and its problems. And threats.

There's some hope, too.

That's a thing that matters to me.

Peter Orullian
January 2015

THE VAULT OF HEAVEN

STORY VOLUME ONE

BATTLE
OF
THE ROUND

INTRODUCTION

ONE OF THE HISTORICAL events in my Vault of Heaven series is called The Battle of the Round. It's the final fight in what's known as the War of the Second Promise. And it's a battle with lasting consequences.

This event is sometimes also referred to as the Battle of the Scar. And "Scar" refers to the Scarred Lands, which is a broad expanse of plains left barren in the wake of this battle. You see, one side of this conflict uses the vitality of living things—the land itself, in this case—to fuel its renderings of the Will, or Resonance. These are magic concepts in the world I've built.

At the center of this story is the notion of sacrifice. Not burnt-offerings and the like. More the personal kind. But taken to an extreme level.

There's also another story center here. It has to do with family, and the willingness to go all in where they're concerned.

That's an idea I like. A lot.

And without lapsing too maudlin, I think part of the idea of "family" in this story includes friends.

I like that quite a bit, too.

1

BATTLE
OF THE
ROUND

MARAL PRAIG KNELT BESIDE the bleeding soldier and examined his wounds. A sword or spear had punctured the man's gut several times. He would die if Maral did not heal him. But to make the lad whole—if it could be done at all—would cost him greatly; he'd have to use much of his own spirit to do it, leaving him with less of that spirit to use in tending to others, men whose wounds were less severe, who might be able to return to the battle right away. He looked down, helpless, into the face of the young man, feeling damned no matter what he chose to do.

Sounds of war filled the air. Metal rang against metal, and the unearthly cries of the inhuman Quietgiven foe unnerved him. The soldier locked eyes with Maral, pain and fear drawing his features tight. But the lad managed to nod perceptibly, lending Maral the strength to push through the clamorous din. Gently, he placed his hand on the soldier's chest, invoked the Will, and caused him to sleep. It took little energy to do it, leaving him still able to tend to many others today.

The lad would die. But at least he would feel nothing as he bled his last.

Maral bowed his head, wondering if the young soldier had a wife, maybe children, and silently hoped he did not.

How many? he thought. *How many have I let die . . .*

Maral raised his eyes and looked around. Several of the Sheason he led were tending the wounds of other injured soldiers. Not for the first time, he questioned his decision to send some of his fellow Sheason to render the Will in battle, leaving others, like himself, to heal those who were wounded. He also felt some small bit of shame that he had chosen to lead from here, instead of from the battlefront.

But he was Randeur of the Order of Sheason, with certain knowledge and authority that he was duty bound to hold safe. He mustn't fall. Still, it did not diminish his feeling that he should be standing with those who, like this soldier lying before him, put their lives at risk.

With his hand still resting on the lad's forehead, a sudden stream of images flashed through his mind, the soldier's dying memories, familiar memories, comforting ones, images of a young boy, maybe five years old, and a little girl just learning to walk. Then a young woman, his wife, smiling at him as he wrestled on the floor of their home with their little ones. She joined the playful fray, which ended in a tender kiss as the children continued to tug at them. He thought he could smell minty beef stew and mild plum wine and hear a chorus of laughter, when abruptly it stopped.

Maral realized he'd shut his eyes as the images filled him. He now slowly opened them to see that the lad's face had relaxed, his struggle over. He looked up again, this time finding the face of his beloved, Laollen, several strides away, a question in her eyes. He shook his head: No, this one . . . this young father . . . was gone. She hung her head in a compassionate moment, mourning with him, her exhaustion and despair mirroring his own; her own Sheason hands were bloody where they rested upon the chest of another soldier felled by war.

Suddenly Maral was overwhelmed by the ache of death, the mounting loss of life, the images in his mind of now-fatherless children, and of parents whose children had perished here.

So much death. For so long. Centuries of war.

He couldn't, he wouldn't, bear it any longer. Inside him, a new feeling began to build: wrath. Without thinking, he stood, turned toward the battle line, and strode purposefully and without hesitation. Calls followed him: his fellow Sheason seeking guidance; his beloved, imploring him to stop. He ignored them all.

Into the fray he went, drawing the Will, releasing the power of his own spirit, and crushing as many as he could of the beastly Bar'dyn that had swarmed south out of the Bourne. He swept his hands in violent gestures at these Quietgiven creatures, forcing them back, casting them high into the air, driving them into the hard soil until their bones cracked.

In some he caused blood to boil, in others to freeze, and at a wall of the unearthly creatures he shot a maelstrom of fire and wind and shards of broken swords and stones.

He cut a path of blood and broken bodies through the battle, seeking King Sechen Baellor, meaning to stand beside the man and draw upon his own life's energy until he could spare no more. He meant for all those who followed him to see that to win, to preserve the lives of those who counted on them, they must let go all restraint and give themselves up to the fury of war.

5

He pushed through another dense line of men who were trading blows with Bar'dyn and other vile beasts he could not name, and climbed a low hill where the king and his most trusted guard stood looking north and west. Exhausted, he yet summoned strength from a reserve he hadn't known he possessed, and pushed through the waves of soldiers and Quiet locked in mortal contest, and finally broke free.

At the top of the bluff he paused and followed his king's gaze. His heart fell.

The land, as far as the eye could see, had been stripped of color and life. Shades of charcoal and desert brown mixed in a miasma of heat and smoke. In the distance he saw dark lines of more Bar'dyn marching toward them. The monsters were inexorable killers, each one stronger than any man.

But the brutish creatures were not responsible for the scorching of the land.

Maral again followed the king's gaze, to a line of dark-robed figures so emaciated that it appeared the wind might blow right through them. They came slowly, creeping over the plain toward the last remnant of Baellor's army.

So many. Where did they come from?

They were velle.

As Maral and his Sheason rendered the Will, so did these Quietgiven wraiths. But the cost of it they drew not from themselves, but from anything living around them.

He looked again at the stripped and barren land. This Bourne army had come much later than anticipated, but for weeks now King Baellor's army had been pushed south and east by the Quiet, constantly retreating, constantly regrouping. Mostly, they fled the unhallowed hands of the velle, who came on slowly, virtually unchallenged, drawing darkly upon the Will to burn and batter Baellor's men and the Sheason who were helping them.

But this . . . their number had more than tripled. There must have been three hundred dark renderers skulking toward them. Had reinforcements recently joined their ranks?

Maral's arms felt suddenly very heavy, and he could see the defeat in Baellor's eyes. They simply could not stand for long against an onslaught of this magnitude.

Several hundred strides from the fray, the velle stopped. Standing in a great staggered line, they faced the vast field of conflict where thousands yet fought as battle calls and iron implements resounded distantly.

As one, the velle got to their knees, like a mass of pilgrims at a temple gate, each raising one bony hand and resting the other on the soil beside it. A sudden tempest leapt from the sky, and the earth heaved. Shards of lightning shot from the heavens, striking down everything they touched. Countless gnashing pits of root and rock opened in the earth, indiscriminately swallowing men and Quietgiven. Bodies flamed or were swallowed by the ground beneath them; others were whirled away like chaff in a high wind.

Will and Sky! He'd never seen the velle coordinate their renderings like this, a blistering display of destruction.

Thousands perished over the next several moments, human and Quiet alike, as the combined renderings of the velle, with their accumulated strength, scoured acre after acre. Half of the king's army was lost. And as Maral watched, the land beneath the velle blackened, the desolation spreading hundreds of strides, as the life inside the soil and all it touched was drained from it.

King Baellor turned a worried look on Maral, who finally dropped to his knees, the effects of his own rendering finally overcoming him. Weak and panting, he pitched forward onto his hands. Baellor motioned for one of his men to help Maral, before leading the rest of his captains in the other direction. They must fall back again. As they retreated, Maral knew it would be for the last time.

CঃৈO

IN THE PALE LIGHT of the moon, King Sechen Baellor knelt on one knee and grabbed a handful of parched, crumbled earth. It had been stripped of color and looked like nothing so much as funeral ash. He lifted it to his nose and inhaled. The soil held none of the familiar loamy smell that he savored in his own garden. It was sterile earth, in which not even the most skillful farmer could coax a seed to grow.

How will I lead an army against this? Their power surpasses that of even the Sheason.

"I thought we had ridden far enough to be past this ruined soil." He let the dirt fall between his fingers, charcoal dust slowly wafting up into the moonlight.

"It spreads," Maral Praig replied, the Sheason offering his king counsel as dark hour approached. "The taint of their rendering goes deep and wide. The effects of this day aren't through."

"I have ordered the lands behind us burned," he told the Sheason. "Since they won't draw their own spirit to render the Will, perhaps we can take away their source. There will be little left that they might use. Tomorrow will be a better day."

His friend said nothing to that.

"It's quiet," Baellor noted softly. "We've not had a night of peace for longer than I can remember. I fear it bodes only ill."

His friend looked away to the north and west, where a few leagues distant the Quiet had uncharacteristically paused in their advance. "They observe their own dark, unholy day."

Baellor stood and looked toward the enemy, finding the faintest hint of fireglow on the horizon. "For what?" he asked.

"They observe the anniversary of the day of Quietus's Whiting. Their god was not always as he is now." His counselor raised his gaze higher still to the night sky above. "In honor of the day he was marked, turned utterly white, they remember him." The Sheason shut his eyes and breathed deep. "When they come again, they will come, I fear, with renewed purpose."

Baellor laughed softly into the solemn quietude. He couldn't help himself. "Because they've only been flirting with us thus far."

The Sheason offered a slight grin, and the two men shared the briefest respite from their failing war.

The smile slowly faded from Baellor's lips. "This is our last stand, my friend. There is little more we can do. We lost half our men today. The convocation committed everything, every available man from every realm that answered the call. When we are gone, no one will remain to resist them. All that will be left of us is this . . . scar." He swept a hand out over the stripped and barren landscape.

Baellor thought about the Convocation of Seats—rulers from almost every realm and nation, summoned to form a mighty alliance. If they failed here in what he felt were the last days of this war, the people it had been called to serve would be left with nothing but this wasteland.

9

"What of General Stallworth?" the Sheason asked. "Any word?"

Baellor shook his head. "He would have joined us by now. No. He fell beneath the heels of this army long before they entered our lands. May the Sky have received him."

"Send word to Y'Tilat Mor," Maral suggested. "Perhaps they will now be convinced to come to our aid. We will need the power of their song to win here. The Mor Nation Refrains may be our last hope."

Baellor's heart was empty. . . . But a king is not allowed to lose hope. "They will not come. We must think of another way."

"And you've no word from across the Soren Seas?" His counselor turned and looked south.

"The ships have not returned. Perhaps the old stories are only that. Perhaps there *are* no nations beyond the shore. No sympathetic races as the stories claim." He drew another deep breath. "Regardless, they would not arrive in time. I sent those ships not to return with help, Maral. I sent them to preserve something of us, should we fall . . ."

It was the Sheason's turn to offer a mild laugh. "You might have given me a chance to go with them."

"Almost went with them myself," he said, his own smile returning.

They then fell into a troubled silence, alternately looking off at the horizon where the plague out of the Bourne rested, keeping their unholy celebrations, and then up into the firmament, where stars offered some small comfort.

Baellor broke the silence with a question and request he wished he did not have to voice. "I've thought of a way," he said.

"To defeat them?" the Sheason asked, without turning.

"Yes. But it requires you to break a vow."

"You want us to draw our strength to render from the land, as the velle do," his friend and counselor said, voicing his sovereign's thought.

Baellor did not immediately speak. He needed Maral to consider this, but he knew he must tread lightly. Even in the extremity of war to which they'd been pushed, it was heresy to ask this.

"Only until we have either sent them to their earth or pushed them back where they came from." He paused, considering. "I know what I am asking."

"Do you?" Maral replied. "Some might tell you that the only thing that separates Sheason from velle is the unwillingness to render by using the world around him—"

"Not forever," Baellor interrupted gently. "Our swords are outnumbered more than ten to one, and would not be enough, in any case, to stand against these velle. We need you and those who follow you to do more." He raised a hand to forestall argument. "We are grateful for your presence: the healings, and those who do fight among us. But you saw what happened today. Things have changed. We can't afford to have your Sheason resting to regain strength before returning to battle as they do now. If they can restore themselves by calling up the strength of the land, as our enemies do . . ."

"If we do as you ask, then we will have betrayed the principles that we came first to defend."

"If we are defeated, no one will be left to debate those principles!" Baellor countered, more angrily then he'd intended.

His friend stared back at him for a long time before saying more. When he did, there was real fear in his voice. "It is not wise to tempt us so. Use of the Will without consequence, even once, makes us indistinguishable from those we stand against." His friend heaved a sigh. "Some of those velle who walk with them even now . . . were once Sheason. It is a thin line we walk. Do not ask this of us."

Unbelieving, Baellor stared back at Maral, who now looked weaker than he ever remembered seeing him. And yet, what alternatives did they have?

Finally, he gave his old friend another smile. "Then we will have to find another way. But I will say this now, since there may not be time later. I have been glad to count you a friend."

He clapped Maral on the back, and left him staring off toward the far horizon, his face a study of weariness and worry.

CRESO

MARAL WAITED AN HOUR, recalling every memory and story he could about the Quietgiven and their solemn observance of Quietus's Whiting. He couldn't help but feel that perhaps hidden somewhere in their ceremonial observance of this day lay key information that might help his king. But nothing came to mind, save the one thing his friend might have asked, but had not: a father's vengeance for his son—almost two years ago now, Baellor had lost his firstborn to this war.

But the king had not spoken of his own loss. Not tonight, and not once since he had taken the field himself. Still, Maral had felt it, as he had the passing of the lad earlier that day. As much as Baellor mourned the passing of his kingdom, he mourned what defeat here would mean for his own family, what it had *already* claimed.

Before Maral knew what he was doing, he was moving beneath the lesser light which had passed into the western night sky, stealing toward the encampments of the enemy.

He cautiously stole over the dark terrain. As he progressed, he caught the scent of fire on the wind. He couldn't tell whether it belonged to the camps ahead or the lands his king was having burned far behind. Or whether, perhaps, it belonged to the hardened soil that lay unnaturally scorched and barren beneath his feet. As he made his way north and west, he felt as though he passed through a new hillock, one littered with bodies that had been left where they had fallen.

Before coming into sight of the Quietgiven army, he summoned a small measure of the Will to cloak himself, blurring his form so that it would seem like no more than a shadow. As he drew nearer, the familiar smells of fire were joined by those of roasting meat and unwashed skin. And now he heard the occasional sound of a deep voice. But not argument or grumbling or the rise and fall of a braggart's tale. These sounded like the fireside conversations he might have with members of his own order; like the exchange he'd had a few hours ago with King Baellor on the long plain.

For all the ferocity and malice he'd seen and heard from these hordes, these were not the tones of the mindless.

As Maral drew nearer still, he bent close to the earth and crept along, moving behind stands of bare-limbed trees or rock formations to keep himself hidden. With care, he edged closer. It occurred to him that if he pulled forward the hood of his robe, he looked, himself, like nothing so much as a velle.

It would be a grave risk to go in alone, but before he could reconsider, Maral let go the energy he'd been using to obscure himself, pulled up his cowl, and stepped out from behind a stand of dead oaks. He strode slowly, but with a measure of self-assurance, to the outer encampment. He kept his head down and his face averted from those who might take note of him.

He hadn't gone far before he caught sight of several velle moving in a slow line to the left, where they disappeared over the lip of what appeared to be a broad gulley. He followed, passing close to several Bar'dyn, who nodded deferentially to him as he walked by. Maral returned the acknowledgment just enough to show he'd seen them.

Shortly, he came to the edge of what stretched out to become a large, shallow basin. When he raised his eyes to survey those settled in here for the night, his heart fell as it had earlier that day at the sight of the many dark renderers.

Sitting in small groups across the dry basin, huddled forward around small fires, were hundreds of men, and women . . . and children. From where he stood it appeared that their hands and feet were bound. Many wore makeshift bandages, as if having nothing save their own clothes to bind their wounds.

Occasionally, a weak cry rose up into the night from among the multitude of prisoners here—some agony getting the better of one or another of them. The cries came mostly in the high-pitched voices of the young.

If the prisoner camp had held only men, he might have understood how they came to be here, likely being captured in battle.

But women? Children?

He spent several moments surveying the host of captives. As he did, he thought he might later remember nothing as much as their slumped shoulders. These people looked defeated, bereft of hope, as though they could only mark the hours until their death.

Maral knew he could not possibly reclaim so many.

Forgetting the care he'd taken to keep his face hidden, he straightenend up, raised his head to stare and wonder if he'd found the key he'd come looking for. If these prisoners would be some kind of sacrifice on this unholy Quiet day.

His heart ached when he saw the small ones held close by mothers and fathers who had no balm for their fear. He grieved as much for those parents who, to allay these children's worries, would choose between a lie and the brutal truth.

He despaired. Until . . .

The wrath he'd felt earlier in the day, when he'd let another brave man die, returned, filling his heart and mind. For a moment, prudence kept him standing there, sure that any attempt to redeem these captives would result in a great many deaths.

His limbs began to tremble with anger as he recalled the faces of hundreds he had healed and sent back into battle. Finally, his last bit of reason was swept aside and with only a vague purpose he descended into the shallow basin.

Before he reached the bottom, a clear deep voice called to him. "You there."

Maral paused, keeping his focus ahead and away from the speaker.

"Where are you going?" the creature asked, using a Bourne tongue that Maral hoped he knew well enough.

"To check the prisoners," he managed, keeping his voice low and slurred.

He heard footsteps approach. He tensed, readying the Will to strike, but knowing it would be futile, as he would fast be overcome by their sheer numbers.

But the velle glided past him, moving toward the closest fire, toward the nearest . . . captives. As the demon neared, the men and women shrank away, their gaunt, tired faces tightening with panic. A pallid hand extended from the robe, reached down, and took hold of the wrist of a girl of maybe six years old. The child looked back over her shoulder at a couple Maral assumed were her parents. When the father tried to rise, the velle raised its other hand.

"*Dal nolle soche shil farran yeae.*" The cryptic words fell from its rank lips in a husky voice, dropping the man back to the ground, his eyes closed.

The girl began to weep weakly.

Then the child's mother rose and threw herself at the dark renderer's arm, trying to break its hold on her daughter. Screams and cries rose up from around the camp. The velle shoved its free hand into the woman's hair and yanked her head back hard. Then it drew her face up close to its own and inhaled slow and long. Maral couldn't be sure, but he thought he saw something like steam pass from the woman's mouth into its nostrils. The woman cried out, her voice steadily weakening. Soon, she slumped and fell back into her daughter before dropping to the ground beside the man. The velle held a bitter grin on its pale emaciated face and raised its chin, shrieking at the multitude of captives, its shrill cry more than a warning. The sound echoed horribly, at once silencing and stilling the countless mass of helpless victims. They were able only to watch and listen.

Then the velle turned back toward Maral, whose own anger had risen again as he observed the child, who stood looking down at her mother at her feet and weeping openly.

He forgot himself entirely and raised his right hand, turning it palm up, receiving the Sky in token, then balled his other hand into a fist and held it out toward the malefactor.

"To the dust!" he said, his voice filled with rage.

He could feel other velle behind him. He would die, even if he could put down this one. But he no longer cared. If for nothing but this single awful act, he would see the demon destroyed.

He let loose the Will, the raw emotion shooting forth with its own terrible force at the creature. He focused it, pushing it at the beast's head. It was all the power left in him after the events of the day, but it was still considerable.

But in that moment, the velle tightened its hold on the child's wrist, and her body began to slacken. Her eyes, though . . . he would never forget her eyes. They widened, seeming to look far away, to see something awful and frightening. Perhaps it was only the agony of losing her own soul, of having it rendered into something new and destructive. He would never forget the fear and helplessness in the girl's face.

The Quietgiven renderer seemed briefly to stand straighter, its body more robust. With a dark smile, it simply lowered its other hand, and all the energy of Maral's attack diffused to nothing more than a slight breeze. Then it yanked the child's arm hard, and in an instant she dropped to the dry earth, desiccated, dead. The velle then raised a hand and brought a sudden pressure to bear on Maral's head. Wind whipped around him, as though he were caught in a tight, choking vortex.

His body was being pressed in from all sides. He felt as if bones were ready to snap in his arms as he held them up to shield his face.

To the earth I return.

But before the pressure became too great, he heard a resounding cry—"No!"—and the pressure stopped.

17

Maral lowered his hands to see a young man, perhaps sixteen, toppling the velle. The boy had run at the renderer and driven it to the ground.

With unlikely gracefulness, the demon rolled and came up with its talon-like hand around the lad's neck. It hissed at him, then immediately turned again to face Maral. As they came around, all the fear he had known before seemed as nothing, when he saw that the boy was his son, Talan.

"Dear Sky, no," he said, his voice failing.

How had they gotten Talan? Why was he here?

"I couldn't let him, Father. I couldn't—"

Before he could consider it more, the velle squeezed the boy's throat, choking off his words. Then it focused its gaze on Maral, a hint of dark amusement on its lips. In that moment, Talan's eyes began to shut, his body slump. The velle raised two fingers toward Maral and the vortex resumed, pressing in on him more savagely than before.

He tried to push it back, but his strength seemed all but gone. He managed to watch as his son's life ebbed slowly beneath the touch of the velle. Talan tried to show Maral a brave face, but he knew his son. The boy was terrified. He also knew that the lad, himself on the path of study to become a Sheason, understood what was happening to him.

He was helpless. He would die. Unless Maral did something to save him.

Unlike the young man today that I let go. . . .

Maral saw in his own beleaguered mind the quiet bravery of the man earlier that day who had been willing to die so that others could return to fight these Quietgiven. He recalled his king who would not speak of his own lost son. And then he looked back at his own dying child. He knew he could not let the valor of all these be in vain.

With all the strength he could find, he pushed back the on-slaught of the velle's rendering and jumped aside, falling hard to the earth. The force he'd thrown off struck the ground and tore a gaping hole where he'd been standing, the impact sending great rocks and sprays of dirt and ash into the air. Maral couldn't be sure, but he thought he also sensed something of his son in the dissipating attack, as though the boy's rendered spirit lingered like a fading residue of the velle's assault.

The velle stepped over the small family that lay heaped at its feet, dragging Maral's son along as it started toward him. Maral had little left to give. He had to choose between one last rendering of the Will and the strength he'd need to try and make it back to his own army. Escape was a foolish notion, he knew—there were so many Quiet around. But he had a simple choice: fight or run.

He had rolled onto his back, readying the Will a final time, when a swarm of bodies descended on the velle, and more yet upon those dark renderers standing on the low embankment to his right. The captives, hobbled as they were, had stood, shuffled toward their captors, and thrown themselves physically upon the velle, stacking atop them like cordwood laid up for winter.

"Run!" his son shouted.

Maral stood, feeling weak and confused as he looked out over the hundreds who stood watching, their vacant eyes now lit, he thought, with the vaguest spark of hope.

It was only then that his mind allowed him to see, that it showed him the lie that, until this moment, he'd managed to tell himself about this camp of prisoners: they were his own, almost all of them. Some were the families of Sheason, others were residents of their city, Estem Salo, that he and his fellows had left behind when they came east to answer the convocation's call.

By my last Sky.

His mind called forth images of his home, the city of Sheason, nestled high in the mountains of the Divide, consumed by flames; of dissenters executed with the wave of a rendering hand; of the generations of knowledge and wisdom, stored in the Archives of Estem Salo by his people, likely now seized or destroyed by the Quiet.

May our safeguards have held our secrets. . . .

Maral looked at his son, whose eyes drooped even as he struggled against the grip of the velle. He had been blind. They all had. These races out of the Bourne—Bar'dyn, velle, all of them—had come to war with more than bloodlust. He saw clearly now the true strategy of the Quiet, allowing peoples to mobilize, while leaving precious things unguarded as they built armies.

The dark irony was that even in their collective strength, the nations of the known world were utterly overmatched.

He thought he now also understood why it seemed the Quiet army had come later than they'd expected: Among, perhaps, other stops, they'd gone to Estem Salo.

And this current assault was the last insult to be heaped upon the resistance of the nations, but more ironically, on the Sheason themselves: that the renderings of the Quiet when they met Baellor's last stand would be made by stealing the life from their enemies' own dear ones. It was more than an insult; it was a terror tactic intended to weaken the resolve of those who followed.

"Run!" his son shouted again, then fell to his knees.

Maral stole one last look at his boy, then at the hundreds standing across the shallow valley, and turned and ran. As he did, it felt as if something inside him broke.

Just to fight one more day.

He clawed his way up and out of the basin, and raced blindly out across the scorched, barren plain, heading, he hoped, in the direction of his king and those Sheason who yet remained.

His lungs burned. Exhaustion threatened to tumble him to the ground. But he kept his legs beneath him, as he tried to think of what to do next. How could they hope to stand against them? Would he have to renounce his oath?

Perhaps oaths, too, have a breaking point.

The very thought intimated a path he was not sure, even now, that he could follow.

CʒꙄꙊ

EVERY LAST MAN OF Baellor's army, now perhaps only twenty thousand strong, stood silent and still in the light of predawn, waiting. Scouts had brought word that the Quiet were on the move early. Baellor stood in front of the line, the point of his sword in the hard dirt, his hands resting on its pommel. He scanned the horizon for the enemy, knowing they would come rested and—as Maral had counseled—with a renewed sense of purpose. His own men were tired and fearful, particularly after yesterday's demonstration of the velle's power.

His strategy to rob the velle of their source to render the Will had failed; they had brought their own. There was nothing more to do but see this out to the bitter last. Messages had already been dispatched to Recityv to evacuate that city. Additional messengers had been sent to the other realms and nations, carrying notes for those peoples to take care for their own safety. As he watched for signs of the enemy, Baellor imagined the years ahead: Quietgiven hunting down mankind, since no military force remained to stand against them; a lawless world, one that accepted the sacrifice of innocent life to enable their dark arts. He would almost be glad to be dead when the world he envisioned came into being.

But more than anything, he would like to have had one more day with Elonas and Olara, his wife and lone surviving child. Too seldom does a king take care to mark the important moments with his own family. It was an error he welcomed the chance to correct. But in his heart, he held no hope of it.

To his left stood Maral Praig, Randeur of the Order of Sheason, a ceaselessly critical and faithful counselor . . . a good friend. In the night, Maral had been to the camps of the enemy, and escaped. His face looked haunted, and a bit uncertain, in the weak grey light. This morning, not a man or woman from his order remained behind the front line—no one would be healed of wounds today; all stood with Baellor's men, their eyes trained ahead. And though these Sheason appeared more weary than the men of sheath and steel, they gave not a single step, standing as far forward as the rest.

The blue hues of morning blurred the scars of the landscape around them, but could not hide the stark contrast of earth and sky, nor banish the smell of blood, or the blighted earth, stripped of color and life. A clear sky slowly surrendered its stars to the coming of day, and the distant sounds of heavy feet rose on the air.

The calm of the moment was almost painful in its suggestion of the violence soon to follow.

Baellor kept a firm forward gaze. *Let this be my last testament: that I would not run or yield, even when no hope remained. . . .*

In the hour that followed, the Quiet drew ever closer, slowly coming into clear view. The enormity of the Quietgiven army disheartened many of his men, who unwittingly uttered sounds of despair. The columns of Bar'dyn . . . the brigades of the half-breeds . . . and the other races out of the Bourne . . . all of them came on. And leading the wave of creatures were the velle, who brought in tow several hundred of the captives Maral had told him about. Men and women and children heavily bound in lines behind them—the families of these Sheason standing with them.

This disturbed Baellor most of all. He looked over at Maral, who caught his eye and shook his head. The Sheason knew Baellor's mind, and even now silently counseled . . . pleaded with him.

Don't do it, Maral was telling him. *Perhaps there is another way.*

We will see, he thought.

He did not consider it lightly—killing the helpless captives had occurred to him sometime in the small hours of the night. A war tactic: remove their ability to render. But the thought caused him to think of Layosah, the woman who had forced him to remember his own oath and office, who had nearly killed her own child to make him see. There was a kind of betrayal in killing one group of people to save another.

And these are the families of men and women who have died alongside us.

But war had its own rules. When the time came, he would know what to do.

He focused on the advancing Quiet. They did not scream or taunt or wail. These breeds from so distant a place came marching into the vague light of morn making only the sound of their feet upon the soil. Their faces remained placid, their expressions studied, if grotesque. They did not halt or slow. They walked toward them, closing the gap.

Then, a hundred strides away, the velle stopped, their captives still too distant to be recognized. At the far edges of the Quietgiven line, the Bar'dyn continued, coming nearer to Baellor's men. The faces of these creatures hardly changed as they hefted their great weapons and set upon the convocation army.

Steel and leather and wood clashed, grunts and cries rising up in the far east and west of the great plain.

It had begun.

For every Bar'dyn his men took down, Baellor lost two. The line was failing already. He looked ahead at the velle and realized that several had taken captives by the arm and were rendering quietly some protection over the Quiet already engaged. Several of the men and women lay slumped at velle feet, entirely spent.

Seeing it, Baellor decided. *I am sorry, my friend.*

Baellor raised his sword high against the cerulean blue sky and dropped it with a shout, "Let fly!"

Two hundred archers raised their bows, having received their instruction hours ago, and took aim at these human vessels being used for their life's energy. From a chorus of bowstrings, arrows took flight, darkening the sky in a wave as they sped toward their targets.

As he watched it begin to unfold, Baellor felt sick at heart. But before the arrows struck, a gust of wind rose up from the ground and sent the volley over the heads of the captives and into the Bar'dyn several rows behind them. Sechen turned sharply to see the Sheason all with hands outstretched. He caught Maral's eye.

"Fool!" he yelled at the Randeur of the Sheason.

"Not this way!" his friend shouted back.

Before Baellor could say more, the line began to collapse. Bar'dyn had flowed in around the velle and were engaging in battle all up and down the line. Baellor's men fell back or were crushed under great hammers and six-foot blades.

They could not hold. They were being flanked already. In a few moments, there would be no options left. He looked around, desperately seeking a strategy for this last stand, a way to defend their flanks.

Then his eyes lit on the symbol of the Sheason Order sewn to the cloak of one of the renderers close to him: the three rings, one inside the next, all joined at one side.

"Pull back!" he commanded. "Form a great round. No flank. Three men deep. Archers behind the rest!"

His order was repeated by his captains all along the line, and quickly the last several thousand men retreated and pulled themselves into a circle a few hundred strides wide. They managed to keep the Quietgiven in front of them, leaving no flank. Archers worked their bows, firing arrows over the heads of their comrades. War machines fired and reloaded, sending boulders into the densely packed ranks of the enemy.

The physicians who'd come to aid the Sheason had abandoned their needles and gut and taken up spare blades.

In this round, we will battle to the last, Baellor thought, and worked at each Bar'dyn who stepped in front of him.

He didn't know how long they fought, but with each moment, the circle grew smaller, his men falling, others stepping into the breach. Slowly, the number of men dwindled, his soldiers hewn down by an army like none any man had ever seen. He caught glimpses of the velle, who seemed now to bide their time. It did not appear their craft would be needed. Beyond them, the dark columns of Quietgiven stretched without end. By nightfall, nothing would be left of Baellor's army.

He fought on, but hope had gone out of him.

CƷᖰꙆ

THE CIRCLE CONTINUED to tighten. Maral had already lost a number of Sheason. Some had fallen to the sword. Others had rendered their own soul and strength until there was nothing left and they dropped, utterly spent, empty.

Baellor's army gave all they had to the battle, but it would not be enough. He imagined the world that would remain when these valiant men had all been put down. A dark age would ensue, where the only use of the Will would be to corrupt and use and enslave. They would harvest the land until it all looked like this barren waste around them. And then they would have to turn to mankind to fuel their renderings, as they had started now to do.

His mind raced, seeking answers, trying to recall something from the annals of history and the Estem Salo Archives, where he'd studied most of his life. But try as he might, he could recall nothing that might help them. They were simply outnumbered. They hadn't the collective energy or strength to defeat the Quiet this time.

He cast a quick glance at the line of velle standing patiently beyond the battle round, remembering yesterday's awful demonstration of their power, when they all drew upon the Will at once. Then he looked past them at the human captives—their friends and families—who waited to be used. He hadn't told anyone other than Baellor *who* these captives were. He feared it would too dishearten these men and women, or perhaps make them tentative when they must, instead, be bold.

But as he weighed that decision again, he pondered the moment yesterday when many velle had simultaneously rendered, and thought, too, of the velle the night before who had used the life of another to draw on the Will.

The dark images coalesced in his mind, and the seed of an idea took root.

Collective strength. Amplified Will. . . .

"Sheason, fall back!" he called. "Pass the word!" He needed to get the attention of all those belonging to the Order.

Within a few minutes, he managed to bring them together at the center of the great round. All gasped for breath, many bleeding from wounds, others collapsed to their knees. Frightened eyes shone back at him, waiting for him to speak, hoping for wisdom, perhaps salvation. The war raged all around them as the sun climbed high into the morning sky.

Maral turned slowly in a circle and began to speak.

"Individually we are not enough to defeat them," he said. "We must join our efforts."

"Join?" one Sheason woman asked through labored breaths.

He looked her in the eye. "Yesterday I watched as the velle drew upon the Will all at once. They slayed several thousand people in a matter of moments." He stopped, considering that what he meant to ask might not work at all, that it might, in fact, have an ill effect. But they had to try something.

"If each of us renders at the same time, and . . . if we stand together in our own circle, taking hold of one another's hands"—he took two fellows by the hand to demonstrate—"we can produce an act of Will a thousand times greater than any one of us alone."

"How do you know this?" another Sheason asked.

Maral tried to think of how to help them see, his own mind struggling to make sense of it. As he fought through the urgency and confusion, he fastened on the image of the velle, from the night before, who had clutched the child and Maral's own son, and used their souls to power its rendering of the Will.

"The velle have begun to take the lives of others in order to render. I believe we can use the principle of borrowing the spirit of another to expand our own capacity. If we all join together . . ."

He saw wary stares in the eyes of his fellow Sheason.

"When we do this, I believe we will create more than just the sum of our individual abilities; I believe each of us will multiply the sum of the two linked beside him. And in our own circle our strength will expand, allowing us to bring to bear an enormity of Will."

He looked past them to the shrinking outer ring of defense. The plain and the rising hill beyond the round still were black with Quiet moving toward them.

If we do this, are we no different from the velle? Maral answered his own bitter question: The difference was that he asked his fellows to willingly surrender themselves to this action; when the velle sought life to power their use of the Will, they seized it by force.

He then grew as still as he could in heart and mind. He looked around at those Sheason who followed him, who had trusted him.

"Trust me now, as you have before," he called with new confidence and vigor. "We will stand together and each focus on a single act, and send, from this circle, a wave of destruction aimed at the Quiet. And if I am right . . . it will roll like thunder, and drive them into the soil they have trodden and raped."

"And if we kill our own sword bearers? Kill ourselves?" a single, dissenting voice replied.

Maral looked over at the man. Perhaps the time had come to tell them. He looked around at the men and women of the order, gathering them all in a long stare. Would they be undone by the truth? In the end, he decided they had a right to know.

Gently, he shared the identities of the captives who stood bound some few hundred strides away. As he spoke, in some he saw disbelief, in others shock. Many, who were not already kneeling, collapsed to the earth, staring down, grief contorting their faces.

He let them have a moment to fully understand and appreciate what was at stake, and what he proposed.

Then, one by one, those who had fallen to the ground stood. Silent resolve seemed to fill each Sheason, as they began to link hands and form a circle. Maral watched as the inner round took shape. More than a hundred Sheason stood hand in hand, facing inward, eyeing one another as though in farewell. But none spoke. And then, as if by silent agreement, they all lowered their heads in an attitude of prayer. And waited.

Silently, Maral gave instruction, sending it into the thoughts of these friends all joined. *Clear your minds. Allow your spirit to flow without any specific desire or intention to the Sheason beside you. Let it become one with the rest of us. Begin now.*

Almost immediately, a great surge of energy flowed into him. With it came the secrets of those linked to him, the indiscretions, the regrets, the personal triumphs. But these faded quickly, as the pulse of raw power seemed to burn away the individual stories and leave an abundance of spirit and strength like nothing he'd ever felt before.

The heart of a giant, he thought privately.

He waited for the fullness of each renderer's spirit to be offered. Linked as they were now, by hand and mind, he could sense even the most skeptical among them as they felt the collective power and relinquished every reserve of their own soul's strength to the whole.

In the moments that followed, with the sense of power and oneness he felt, there came simultaneously a sense of peace that surprised him.

When the moment seemed right, he spoke again with his mind.

Focus on the velle first. Think upon what you have seen them do, their unhallowed use of the Will. When you have fixed that in your heart, expand your thoughts to the rest of the Quiet, and envision their destruction.

But more than any of this, think of your husbands and wives . . . and children. Of our friends and dear ones who were besieged and taken captive to become the instruments of your destruction. Consider their fear and pain and loss, and let the sorrow of it quicken your indignation.

Then in his thoughts he heard: *Maral. What of Talan?* It was Laollen. This last secret he let go. *Yes, he is with them.*

He allowed the revelation to be known to all, and felt a surging response of thought and emotion and strength as the reality of loss was made personal.

Then take all of me, she said.

A silent chorus of their fellow Sheason said the same.

He spared a last moment to recall the face of a man he had let die so that others could be healed and returned to war; a face that had braved death for that very purpose. The moment passed, but left him filled with indignation. When all was firm in his mind, he raised his face to the sky and screamed out a soul-rending cry that sent forth a flare of light with the radiance of a thousand suns. He felt his body begin to fall, and caught a glimpse of all the Sheason joined to him likewise collapsing, their hands still locked together.

ೲೞ

A MIGHTY SCREAM ROSE up behind Baellor, and a great light blossomed. An enormous boom, deeper by far than any peal of thunder he'd ever heard, rode the wave of light, an inexorable force that moved outward fast. Baellor watched as the blinding flash left his army untouched and passed quickly to the Quiet army. The velle fell first, followed closely by the other Quiet breeds, their bodies sloughing away like sand in a high storm or falling like scarecrows.

It all happened in the space of moments.

He turned then, searching for his friend and counselor, and spotted him lying on the barren soil at the center of the round, his hands clasped to Sheason on both sides. It was the same with all the rest of his friend's fellows, fallen in a circle of their own.

He rushed to Maral's side. His friend was dead. They were all dead. Baellor realized instantly the epiphany his friend had had, the last act of Will to which he'd committed himself.

He put a hand on Maral's forehead. "Thank you."

The scarred lands around them remained silent for a long time, soldiers having sat where they stood, resting, offering gratitude in their own way.

Baellor surveyed the long, wide plain, strewn with countless bodies, the blood having flowed out upon the parched earth. These dead lands struck him as being like a great, open grave.

Then, distantly, hours later, into the stillness and silence came the sound of heavy marching feet. He rose and soon saw from the north more Quiet coming on toward them—rear troops, but without velle. Renewed anger and determination filled his heart.

"Up, lads!" he cried. "For the blood of those fallen here, we will make an end of this."

CఠఠO

THREE DAYS AFTER MARAL had raised his last rendering cry, the army of the convocation put down its last Quietgiven. Those from the Bourne that remained fled back into the north and west. It was only then, with the time to walk the vast fields of this war, that King Sechen Baellor realized the magnitude of the losses, despite the few thousands that had survived. The stench of death had begun to rise. And at the center of the carnage lay a hundred or more Sheason, whose end became, for him, the last, best benediction to the battle of the round.

"Good-bye, my friend," Baellor whispered, his words lost in a dry wind that swept over the scarred lands.

WITH WHAT'S
FAMILIAR

INTRODUCTION

IN *TRIAL OF INTENTIONS*—book two of The Vault of Heaven—there's this king. He's called the smith king. His city is filled with blacksmiths and gearsmiths who are in constant manufacture of the instruments of war.

But it's not a city of forges that gives him his moniker. Rather, it's because this king was once a smith himself. And after I introduced him in the book, I knew I had to go back and write the story of how a blacksmith becomes king.

Don't get me wrong. The way our smith king has evolved the craft of war gives me tingles. There's some of this in *Trial of Intentions*. And a lot more on the horizon. But his origin story wasn't about glory in battle as a sword-wielding titan.

No, this guy won with smarts. With engineering. With the good application of a hot brand.

I also wanted to write a story in my world with a sense of humor. Where in the midst of the grim events taking place, a friendship could have some smiling.

The other thing that happens, is that the young man you see here is not the same man you find in the book. In *Trial of Intentions*, he's older. Hardened. At least until one of my most irreverent characters shows up . . .

WITH WHAT'S FAMILIAR

THE SWEET SCENT OF sawdust mingled with the tang of
hot iron on the air of twilight. Twilight. Jaales Relothian's
favorite hour to work. Just him, alone with the tools and forge
coals and stacks of shore-cut timber. In those quiet hours, when
the hours of war receded and men slunk back to rest and lick
their wounds, he could take his time. Time to craft with cedar
or bent iron what things he could imagine. The shape of a thing
could be found if one had the patience to find it. Iron, heated and
worked at with the right hammer, could become a useful tool or
weapon, if that's the need. Wood, set to with a sharp saw and a
good knife, might become a walking stick or barn joist or a child's
drum. Getting at the shape of a thing took steady hands. And
time. Jaales Relothian had both.

On this night, he'd conceived of a new forge hammer, one fashioned
all of one material. No separate handle. The notion intrigued him.
If nothing else, it'd make a better weapon in his training sessions.
In fact, those sessions had inspired the design.

He'd just drawn out a bit of orange-hot iron, when the dark
shapes of three men brushed through the cedars.

Their scarlet uniforms were deeply soiled. Despite that, even in the twilight, Alon I'tol *reds* were striking. And the lion insignia, woven with simple lines into their tabards was still discernible. The man on the left clutched his arm, blood on his fingers and staining his sleeve. On the right, an elder-looking man supported a third, who shuffled with a gimpy leg. This last soldier had fresh blood stains near an angry slice in his trousers.

They came to a stop, the older man offering a wan smile in the half-hues at end of day. It was Captain Delaquah, his hair more salt than pepper. And his stubbly beard lending him a gruff appearance.

"Come to ask another courtesy?" Jaales said, returning the man's smile.

The old, shared joke brought an easy laugh from the captain. "I break 'em. You repair 'em."

"I'm not a physick man. Nor a surgeon. I have no remedies." Jaales responded by rote. Their exchange had become a kind of steeling to what would follow.

"I have men deft with needle and gut, if that was the need." Delaquah turned regretful eyes on these two of his men. "I'd have preferred they fight over the storied beauty of Lakmi Gopal. Terrible flirt they say. Kind of woman whose hollow promises a man is apt to let himself believe."

Then the captain of this Alon I'tol brigade looked back at Jaales, the humor gone out of him. No smile left for their meeting banter. "I could have 'em sewn up, but there's real work ahead. Gut-stitch won't hold a man together when it begins. I need their cuts closed up permanent."

"My coals are hot," Jaales said, finishing the familiar exchange.

With that, Delaquah helped the gimpy soldier forward, and onto a sturdy oak table. Experience and use had seen several lashes fitted into the wood, to tie down a man's arms and legs. Against convulsive reactions. Once the fellow was secured and his trouser leg cut away, Jaales brought out a stemmed length of birch. He explained its use by simply placing it between his own teeth so the solider could see and understand. Then he placed it gently into the man's mouth, offering him a look of reassurance. And a nod.

While Delaquah stood close, holding the lad's hand, Jaales retrieved a narrow length of iron, one of a few he placed on the coals at day's end—every day—for cases like this. There'd been many. Many because the first time he'd met Delaquah—the captain coming to him with this same request—Jaales's hand had never hesitated. Or trembled. It had forged their friendship, so to speak.

"Prepare yourself." Jaales reached down and picked up a bottle of wood alcohol. He liberally doused the long cut over the man's thigh, washing it clean. The solider closed off a yelp almost before it had begun, his leg tensing to show long, lean lines of muscle.

A moment later, on the mild air of twilight, rose a sizzling noise as Jaales applied hot iron to flesh. The lad didn't scream around his makeshift bit. He let a brief grunt, then tensed again, this time every muscle in his body strained against the pain.

Jaales hated the smell of burnt flesh, but he didn't let it distract him. With one hand he held the wound closed, and with the other he pulled a slow, steady path with the iron tip, cauterizing the cut to the last ragged bit of torn skin. Finished, he bent close to inspect the raw, angry looking line of burnt tissue. Satisfied, he doused it again with alcohol and wrapped it with some fresh bandages laid close by for times like this.

Delaquah untied the straps and assisted the lad down from the table. He laid him up under a bushy cedar tree, where the solider passed out from some combination of exhaustion and shock.

Then, they repeated the process. The second man bore down on the birch bit, grunting around it as his wound was sealed up. When his injury had been bandaged, he nodded thanks and strolled slowly from Jaales's forge and carpentry area, disappearing back toward the encampment of tents.

Left alone with Delaquah in a darker shade of twilight, Jaales offered the captain an ironic grin.

After a long moment, the man shook his head and chuckled. "That's what I like about you. Nothing can stop your smiling teeth. What's the joke tonight?"

"I'm the king's first traveling smithy. His first that can also lay out a trebuchet frame." Jaales laughed. "And I suspect my greatest value to you is branding soldiers. This is hardly what I signed up for."

"You're wrong," Delaquah said, smiling but serious.

"Yeah, then tell me what you think of my swordwork." he countered. It was a small barb at the man, with whom he spent time each day in field-practice. He trained with sword and *hammer* of all things. A smith hammer. Because the captain's philosophy was that you fight with what's familiar.

"I mean you're wrong about your value." The man looked off in the direction of the siege fields. "Light's gone today. Meet me at dawn at the far edge of the encampment."

With that, Delaquah touched a finger to his temple and then swung it forward toward Jaales. Not a formal salute. More a gesture of respect. Acknowledgment. Then he ambled into the shades of evening, humming something tunelessly as he went.

Jaales didn't waste another precious moment of twilight, returning to his new hammer design, losing himself in the rhythms of pounding hot iron.

C3880

"WHAT DO YOU SEE?" Delaquah asked.

Jaales stood with the captain a hundred strides west of the tent line, staring toward the Lonmarck hills and the city of Graas. Behind them, light slowly strengthened in the east.

"It doesn't look like limestone." he said first, anxious to begin their sparring.

"Limestone?"

"We passed a quarry a few leagues back. On our way from Ir-Caul. I assume it's where Graas harvested its city stone," Jaales explained.

"Hmmm," Delaquah grunted, then fell silent, waiting. Clearly Jaales was missing something.

He looked north and south along the outer city wall, raised of a darker stone than he'd ever seen used for city walls. It could have been black marble, but that was expensive rock. And to his knowledge the nearest quarry was more leagues away than was practical for city walls. A material for a king's hall—and purse—maybe, not ramparts and battlements.

A few moments later, perhaps with a hint more light in the sky, he truly saw. "They've raised a layer of timber over the stone."

"Thick. And fresh cut," Delaquah added.

"More yielding to the payloads we hurl with our siege gears," Jaales finished. "Smart."

"And the Nallanians must have a thousand archers on those walls. More ballistas than I can count. Crossbowmen. It's hell trying to get close enough to raise a tower."

"Smart," Jaales repeated. He'd seen a lot of recent harvesting of birch and maple in the surrounding forests. Now he knew why. "But even green wood will eventually break."

"True," Delaquah admitted. "But my instinct is we're outmanned already. We can't dig in for a long one here. Our only option is to take the city fast."

The pause that followed might as well have been a spoken request. Invitation. Delaquah wanted Jaales's thoughts on how to tackle the problem of the wood barrier. Not a surprise really. Over the last year or so, he'd spent more evenings than he could count chatting with the captain, mulling over knots in strategy, logistics, and even politicking back up the chain to the King's trust. Whatever he lacked in swordcraft, Delaquah apparently felt he made up for in logic. The man never said it outright, but he'd taken Jaales as something of a counselor.

Today, they fought the Nallanians at Graas, an Alon I'tol city their perennial enemies had recently seized. A month ago, they were battling Nallan troops in the rocky plains of east of Sever Ens. And a year ago they'd spent six cruel winter months at the brink of the Mal Wood defending against a northern invasion by a treacherous Nallan force bent on annihilation. Not occupation.

Delaquah had been embroiled in countless more battles in the endless war with Nallan. The feud stretched back through the annals, taking fresh meaning with each generation's sense of pride and feelings of being slighted. Footmen happily paid the price for those feelings. The hatred and distrust was pervasive and mutual between the two kingdoms.

"So, it's a stall tactic," Jaales observed. "A prolonged siege will succeed against the timber, but in the meantime, you lose men, animals." He looked at Delaquah with added meaning. "Your resolve wanes. And they've occupied Graas with an army probably three times the size of this company."

Looking again, Jaales could now see arrows buried in the wood, and scorch marks.

"You've tried to burn it. But those would be easily doused with buckets from the rampart walk." He squinted, focusing on one section of the wall. "It's thick, too, isn't it?"

Delaquah made a grumbly noise in his throat. "I'll tell you what I hate most." He fell silent, his anger weighing on the air. "Nallan occupiers take only one type of prisoner. Women. And those are made sport of. Sexed until Nallan seed takes root in their bellies. The rest . . . men, children." He shook his head. "And here we are throwing rocks at sticks."

Delaquah turned to look back at the encampment of his brigade, while Jaales stayed focused on the wall. "What do I do, Smith?"

Despite the fact that his name was Jaales Relothian, when Delaquah addressed him as Smith, it was more personal, more intimate somehow. His plea came limned with a brand of respect he'd only ever seen the man pay once. And quite some time ago.

Staring at the wall, he thought it through. His first idea was iron balls with spikes to tear at the wood on impact. But there was a good chance they'd simply stick. And he didn't think they'd have the sheering force he imagined they'd need to rip the wood apart. He moved past several other notions of impact and blunt force, returning to the idea of fire. Lit arrows obviously hadn't worked. And green wood was hard to burn. But fire was the key.

After a several long moments, a grin spread on his face. "Did you know," Jaales said, casual as you please, "that I'm also a glassblower."

Delaquah turned to see him smiling, the confusion on his face turning to interest, and confidence, though he could have no idea what Jaales had in mind.

CႩ8O

TWILIGHT HAD PASSED when the captain brushed through the trees into the small clearing where Jaales stilled worked at his new hammer design. No wounded soldiers came with him tonight, and Delaquah himself wasn't limping, though his step was slow. Slower than usual. By degrees, his face took shape in the twilight as he came into the light of the lamps.

The man carried something in front of him, held low by his hips. He was staring down at it when he stopped a few paces away. "I need more mending tonight," Delaquah said, in his voice an attempt at levity that he clearly didn't feel. The words fell flat around the forge and ingots and shorn logs.

Jaales said nothing, staring at the broken sickle in the man's hands, the blade broken along its circling swoop. "It's easily fixed," he said with reassurance.

"The weapon, yes. You'll patch it up good as new, I know." He looked up, a weary smile on his face. "I break 'em. You fix 'em, remember."

Jaales pointed down at the sundered weapon with his new hammer which glowed faintly orange at the tip. "Then why the mourner's frown. You walk like a man bearing a pall."

Delaquah sighed heavily, shaking his head as if to clear it. "Dispatch arrived. The king is ill. It's serious. We could wind up in succession any day now."

"Then we'd better get your sickle ready. You'll be first among those asked to fight for the signet." Jaales came around his anvil to retrieve the broken weapon, feeling a bit of excitement. In Alon I'tol, when one king went to his earth, the next was chosen by battle. Worthy successors put up a claim. Typically, one seeking the throne would have earned reputation enough that the claim made easy sense. Then, those who sought to be king fought for the privilege. The wisdom went that the best man would defeat the rest, with some mix of both strength and cunning.

The captain shook his head as he handed the two halves of the curved blade to Jaales. "Fight with the familiar. For me, that's sword and sickle. Did I ever tell you why?"

Jaales didn't immediately reply, taking time to carefully place both parts of the curved blade in his coals. When he returned, he gestured with a bit of flourish. "Now tell me your tale."

Delaquah chuckled and scrubbed his face, seeming to want to scrap off the grit of battle. "I'm not from Alon I'tol. And that there is more than a threshing blade to me." He pointed toward his sickle abed the coals.

Jaales placed his hammer-in-progress into a dousing bucket, and leaned back against a saw-horse he used to measure and cut lengths of wood. He was settling in to hear a story.

45

The captain smiled. "Not much to it, really. I came north as a young man. Seeking reputation, if I'm honest. Was good with my hands. Good like you. But for tearing things apart not putting them together." He paused, sighing again, but gently this time. "I'm from Risill Ond. We're a harvest people. Crops down to our bones. But there's a streak of fight in us, too. You've heard the old stories about the Reapers of Risill Ond, I'm sure."

Jaales had. A contingent of men who'd marched from beyond Recityv clear to the Darkling Plain to throw in with the few Sedagin against an onslaught out of the Bourne. They were the only small country to answer the call. So called "reapers" because they carried sickles—the instrument of their threshing fields. But Jaales mind ran past the old stories, piecing together bits of what he'd just seen and heard: Delaquah shaking his head, the king falling ill, succession soon. "You can't fight to bear the signet, can you?" he said, feeling a bit indignant at the idea. "Because you're foreign blood."

"I'd prefer to fight over the storied beauty of Lakmi Gopal. Terrible flirt they say. Kind of woman whose hollow promises a man is apt to let himself believe." Delaquah smiled at his own joke.

Jaales didn't play along tonight, waiting quietly for the man to say more.

After his smile faded, the captain's eyes turned back to Jaales. He nodded. "Because I'm foreign blood. I don't regret that. And I don't hold any bitterness toward the way of succession hereabouts." He fell quiet, shaking his head again with a look of regret.

But there was more, something unspoken in the way he talked about his origins. To Jaales, that *something* was obvious. "Who do you believe will succeed the king? And why does it concern you?"

The grin that rose on Delaquah's face was a familiar one. The captain liked that he didn't have to be explicit about everything with his company smith. But rather than give him a simple answer, he asked, "Do you want to pick up the day's lesson now? I robbed you of it this morning."

Jaales eyed his friend. This might be an evasion of his question, but he did want to practice. So, somewhat reluctantly, he nodded. "What will you fight with?" he asked, indicating the shorn sickle.

Delaquah searched the ground, casting about for a moment until he came upon a hardened cedar root vaguely sickle-shaped. "This'll do."

The man drew his sword and hunkered a bit, an invitation to spar. Jaales picked up the dull blade he used for their training hours, and his forge hammer besides. *Fight with what's familiar.*

With no preamble whatsoever, Delaquah began to run through a series of exaggerated attacks, all at half-speed. The man hadn't yet given Jaales permission to perform any attacks of his own. Instead, every movement he'd been shown was defensive in nature: blocks, parries, avoidances, and a few disarm techniques. Each one was run through at this crawling pace, the captain scrutinizing his every move: the angle at which he held his weapon, his arm and elbow and shoulder positioning, stance, the direction each of his feet were pointing, depth of his knee-bend, waist and hip orientation, the balance of his weight. And on. And on.

It wasn't unheard of that an entire lesson would consist of a single attack, repeated until Jaales's muscles burned like heaven fire. Which was saying something for a smith man, who repeated the same actions all day long.

And that night, the lesson ran twice as long. Delaquah seemed to be burning off some anger and worry. By the end of it, each of them was slick with sweat, and breathing heavy. Over their few hours together, the captain made a hundred small corrections to Jaales's technique. Most of those corrections he'd repeated no less than three times. But no more than three. If Delaquah said something three times, a healthy amount of frustration crept into his face, some disappointment, too. But he wouldn't say it again. He'd simply reset the motion and make Jaales do it slower still, which was hell on the arms and legs, and a great deal more challenging to do in-balance.

When his friend tossed aside his cedar root, Jaales looked down at his forge hammer. Despite the slow learning pace, it was showing signs of wear. Thousands of blocks and parries—steel edge meeting wood handle—gave it the look of a deadfall limb taken to by an industrious beaver. It was precisely this that had given him the idea of a hammer made all of one piece of iron. It'd be heavier to wield, but less susceptible to wear and breakage.

The captain caught him studying the hammer he held. "A man feels more confident holding something he knows how to use."

Jaales looked up, arching his brows a bit. Would he finally hear the full explanation of this battle technique? One, he liked to remind Delaquah, that most of his own men failed to adopt. In a broad sense, *fighting with the familiar* rang with a kind of homey wisdom. And Jaales had gone along with it, since the techniques they studied were mostly dual-handed. For Delaquah, a sword and sickle. For Jaales, a short blade and his hammer. But he'd always felt some deeper meaning to the approach. Every time he'd inquired, though, he'd gotten a stock response, *When you're ready.*

"Am I ready, then?" He laughed out loud, fully expecting his friend to shake off the question.

"My absent gods, I think you are." He wore a half smile, but Jaales could see Delaquah meant it. *Heard* that he meant it, too— his friend rarely cussed the *absent gods*, the storied framers of this world who'd deemed it unfit and left it alone practically before they were done creating it.

The captain strolled in under the roof of the forge and leaned back against the saw horse, folding his arms and staring out at the night.

Jaales took a spot beside him. And the two looked off in the same direction, much the way he and his father had often done when wisdom was about to be shared.

"A man who makes fighting a career . . . that man, if he has coordination in his limbs and the will to practice, he can pick up the use of most any weapon." Delaquah was nodding to himself. "Some few will even become masters with those weapons. A few.

"But most men don't wear a uniform; they're not soldiers. They don't practice every day. Don't live to do battle. Most times, the fight comes to these kinds of men by way of highwaymen or drunken misunderstandings. Chance things. In such a case, can you imagine asking a thresher or miller or chandler to pick up a sword? Would be nonsense."

Jaales agreed with a wordless noise in his throat.

"Success in any bout is eight stones confidence, one stone ability, and one stone luck."

Jaales made a different sound. A questioning kind.

"Don't believe me?" Delaquah laughed, itching his cheek. "Well, I might be exaggerating some. But not much. And only to make my point." He took hold of Jaales arm. "This here. Strong as cold iron from a lifetime of swinging a hammer. And your muscles know the arc and recoil and feel of its momentum. Things you don't have to think about to do expertly.

"They're things you'll trust if pushed to violence. You won't think about them. They'll just be there." He chuckled low in his throat. "I've seen a shepherd put shame to three armed bandits with a good crook. I watched a trawler deckhand use a fish drub to beat off pirates swinging cutlasses. Happy hells, I've even witnessed a high-lace lady push back a cudgel-flailing roller with a parasol."

"And Risill Ond is a land of wheat threshers. So you carry a sickle," Jaales observed, stating the obvious when Delaquah had grown quiet. It was little more than a prompt to continue.

When Delaquah spoke again, it sounded vaguely like a prayer. "Our weapons have a shape. They have a sound. They feel a certain way. They have good uses. And limitations. And it's not just our weapons. It's everything, isn't it?" He looked around. "Even in this makeshift workshop of yours. There's a universe of physical things. Each with properties you know better than any man or woman for a hundred leagues. In my lifetime, I'll never know them so well."

They fell silent again. This time, Jaales didn't rush to fill that silence with sound.

After a time, Delaquah smiled, lightening the mood a tad. "I think it's a good thing."

"What's that?" Jaales asked, hanging on the answer.

The captain raised an eyebrow. "I break 'em. You fix 'em."

"You mean that I can cauterize a wound?" For the first time in he couldn't remember how long, Jaales wasn't following the captain's train of thought.

He shook his head. "That we have these dependencies on one another. That there are things only you know. Things familiar to *you*. Things whose shape and sound and uses you understand. Things that . . . if asked, you could raise in anger. With confidence. That's a good thing."

Jaales knew he'd be sitting up that night, reviewing this conversation. "And what about my swordwork?"

Delaquah's smile held a hint of irritation. "Have you listened to anything I've said? Why do you care so much about your wandering blade?"

Wandering, he'd said. His trainer's term for bad positioning and wasted motion. "That bad?"

"You'll improve," the captain offered with small conciliation.

A companionable silence fell between them, as the cool night air chilled their sweaty skin. Neither made any effort to break the peaceful spell that can often follow a strenuous workout.

But later on, Jaales explained, keeping his voice soft so as not to overly disturb the quiet feeling that had wrapped them like a cocoon. "When I left my father's shop, I thought I was joining a company to fight. I had the idea that my forge-strong arms would make me a good footman. Deadly with a blade." He trailed off, realizing for the first time that he held no real bitterness for how it all had worked out. Some small bit of disappointment, maybe. "When you put me in the rear, smithing . . . I guess I wasn't expecting that."

Delaquah gave him a thoughtful look—the slow, appraising kind that his father used to show just before revealing some smith technique that Jaales was finally ready to understand. Which made the captain's words the stranger, "So, you're a glass-blower, too.

What in all the empty temples does that have to do with the timbered city walls we looked at this morning?"

☙

IF THERE WAS ONE thing Jaales had learned about war, it was that the poems commemorating battle—verse by Hargrove, Toile, even Bentor—were misunderstood. They weren't stanzas romanticizing warfare. Not a damn jot. But then, he conceded, to fully appreciate what they actually were, you probably had to have stood in a forward position where the smell of blood on the cold ground taught lessons about war that reading and theorizing never would.

And those men, Hargrove and the rest, had turned poet later in life, after years spent fighting in one army or another. Of course, there were poets who'd never held a sword. But for whatever reason, truth rang more sharply from the pens of lyricists whose first instrument had been steel. To Jaales's mind, most words set down by other poets read like thinly veiled propaganda—some condemning bloodshed without the benefit of insight; and some extolling glories no footman ever saw, or wanted.

Standing in the small hours of night, those poems ran through his mind. Mostly, because he wondered what the poets would record when they learned of what was about to happen.

The night guard atop the city walls was at its fewest. Not absent, but they'd be dreamy-eyed and unwitting. The Alon I'tol force had yet to attack after dusk or before dawn. Jaales had given instruction for all preparations to be made in the dark. No lanterns, no torches. It was a moonless night, so the goings were especially slow.

Over the preceding week, he'd doubled the number of engines along the line, staggering them in two rows. He'd spent time calibrating their payload distances. And Delaquah had lightened the pressure on the occupiers, engaging enough so as not to be suspicious, but conserving men and resources to follow Jaales's stratagem.

"Are they all loaded?" he asked, his breath a series of dim silver plumes limned by starlight.

"Every one," Delaquah answered. The man's voice came low, but filled with anticipation.

"I'd send several volleys before the archers strike," Jaales suggested. He felt some anticipation of his own, tempered by a healthy portion of apprehension. *I hope this works.*

"We'll adjust the payload slides a hand-length," the captain said, his tone now focused to the task. "Better spread that way."

With no real fanfare, Delaquah signaled the command. In the stillness, the sound of timber payload arms swinging heavily down, and slings whipping up, filled the night. Jaales tracked one of the thick glass balls sailing against the darkened sky. And he caught the flickering outline of several more. All filled with his alchemical mixture: pitch, naft, and quicklime. A few moments later, the sound of shattering glass came in tinny echoes across the long fields.

A few confused shouts rose from the top of the wall, sounding like the bark of dogs heard distantly. Then came the tinkling of glass cascading down the wall. One man on the wall cried out, "Sorcery!" That made Jaales smile.

The men worked quickly to reset the engines, and cast a second set of Jaales's newest creation. The glass balls measured wrist-to-elbow in diameter, the glass itself thick as his thumb. Each one had been filled with the carefully prepared admixture, and sealed. The idea was elegant in its simplicity.

A third and fourth and fifth volley struck the wood barrier. The green birch and spruce would be well sodden by now. As the engine-men set for a sixth volley, a line of archers—a hundred men at least—raised bows and drew arrows tipped with resin-soaked hemp. In the night, sulfur sticks flared, lighting the hemp.

"Aim and release!" Delaquah commanded.

The arrows sailed in long, beautiful arcs, flaming against the darkness. And this time, as they struck the timber, they lit the compound Jaales called *slurry*. The name amused him. In moments, the wall was an inferno, blazing hot and bright like a sheer cliff of fire. Engine-timber creaked again, more glass balls hurled toward the blaze. The shattering glass mingled with the low, rumbling sound of immense flame.

In short order, men atop the wall began trying to douse the flames, pouring water from buckets. But besides being unable to dump water fast enough, each drop caused the fire to flare more brightly. Jaales smiled at his own cleverness: thrice-reduced quick-lime. A material component that, to his knowledge, was his own invention. He'd happened upon it rather by chance in his years spent huddled near forges and kilns.

From this distance, he was forced to imagine the looks of confusion on the Graas occupiers as their efforts only made the fire worse. All the while, Delaquah kept a steady pace of slurry balls flying at the wall.

By dawn, the timbers were little more than charred bits lying at the base of the wall. For the last hour before sunrise, the glass balls had continued to arc against the sky. Now, though, they splattered slurry against limestone brick. And from the wall, black smoke rose in thick waves, ascending the morning blue. It reminded him of autumn fires and the tang of burning leaves.

Delaquah raised an arm. The engines stopped. His company stood still, watching. A quarter hour later, when the flames and smoke had receded, the captain turned to Jaales. His brow rose in silent question. Jaales nodded. Delaquah pointed to a man at the treeline.

From the Lowal river, a stone's throw back inside the forest behind them, men came bearing rounded earthen pots and more glass balls. These had been sitting in the cold waters of the Lowal all night, resting on its sandy bottom. The very sand from which Jaales had fashioned the balls. The poets would make much of this, he imagined. Resonances and rhymes.

Inside these containers swirled a different liquid, malted barley vinegar mostly, a few filled with apple-must vinegar. The engines were loaded with these new payloads. When they struck the scorching hot limestone wall, spraying their contents, the sizzle and hiss rose like a chorus of the fabled Dorma serpents. The ones who awoke every seventeen years and returned to hibernation only after gorging on doubters and fumbling musicians—the two were seen as close cousins.

For another hour, the engines did their work, barraging the wall. The sound of freezing cold vinegar crackling against the fire-hot stone came with the occasional faint pop as wall-stones fractured and mortar slipped.

The sun sat low on the eastern horizon, not yet an hour since dawn, when the engines ceased to fling. The wall had cooled. The men up and down the line were sweating freely from constantly hauling pots and loading slings.

Delaquah let them have a moment to breathe before signaling their third wave. Normal payloads now. Hard granite and some iron balls, besides. But before the first one let fly, the sound of hooves over forest soil rose behind them.

An armed horse company emerged from the trees. Jaales made special note of their armor. Fine quality. Most of these suits had never seen a smith's mend. But the men wearing them weren't fresh on appointment. That much was clear in the look of them. And sure as every hell, the man who led them was no stranger to a siege. Jaales knew the look in this man's features. He'd seen the same look in Delaquah's face. It was the iron expression his captain wore when he held a man down while his wounds were cauterized.

Their leader dismounted, and came around to face Delaquah. The two made a formal clasp of hands, a captain's grip. "Still at it, I see," the man said, a hint of critical grin beneath his beard.

"And in no need of assistance, Mykol." Delaquah cast an exaggerated gaze over the line of horsemen. "Wouldn't want your pups to get dirty."

That fetched a genuine laugh from Captain Mykol. "You always were an enemy of cleanliness."

"And you've always had immaculate timing." It was Delaquah's turn to offer a critical grin. The man looked out at the walls of Graas, now cracked and ready to be broken down. The hour of siege was at hand. If they succeeded in retaking the city, Mykol and company would now be seen as the factor that made it so.

The fresh captain gave Delaquah a chilly look. But the icy expression shifted fast to one of state decorum. "I'm not here to help you fail. I'm here because the king has gone to his earth."

Jaales watched as his captain's face visibly slackened. It was the look of a man who'd held hope of a friend's recovery. Delaquah shook his head. "Damn shame."

Mykol made a show of his own grief, but it looked affected. Could have been that the man had already had his time to grieve, but didn't wish to appear unfeeling. To Jaale's, he rather looked like a man with a plot.

"The king would have wanted us to name a successor quickly. It's dangerous for the body to have no head." Mykol spoke in a softer tone, but sounded more conspirator than confidante.

Delaquah stared blankly back at him. "You."

"I've announced my intent." As if to confirm it, he placed the heel of his palm on the pommel of his sword.

"And likely beaten every challenger," Delaquah surmised, "bringing you here. Into the field. To rush your ass to sit on the throne of bones."

"Steffon was your friend. But he was *my* king."

Jaales understood the slight. Delaquah was a thresher, not born in Alon I'tol. And any king here—so the custom went—would have, upon his death, one of his bones artfully woven into the kingdom's throne. All Along I'tol kings had from the beginning had a bone in that chair, and every bone originating in its homeland. The reasons for the tradition were obscure, but had something to do with reaching back to true origins. Right origins.

A long silence settled over the two companies. Men from each side eyed one another with disapproval and threat and something more. Something Jaales could only think to call the haughty sniff of standing on moral high ground.

Finally, Delaquah broke the silence. "You're half right. He was my friend. *And* he was my king. And *you're* lucky I can't challenge you for the signet, or I would put an end to your personal campaign here and now."

Assuming a kingly posture, Mykol's spoke perfunctorily. "I'm obliged to ask if any of your men feel ripe for leadership. Any man can raise a hand for the signet during succession."

Another silence stretched over the men in lion red. There were mighty fighters among the Delaquah ranks. A few with a knack for leadership, too. None of them stepped forward.

Mykol smiled with satisfaction and turned back toward his horse, when Delaquah did nothing more than raise an arm and point. At Jaales.

Delaquah didn't look at Jaales. Didn't speak. He merely waited for the would-be king to acknowledge his gesture. Mykol had nearly mounted before noticing his men all staring in a single direction. He followed their gaze to Jaales, who in turn stared at Delaquah.

What in the name of every absent god is he doing?

Jaales shot a look at Mykol, who was clearly irritated. The man began removing his cloak, presumably in preparation to fight. Delaquah lowered his arm and strolled—actually strolled!—over to Jaales. He took a position beside him, much as he'd done the night he'd explained his combat technique, and spoke with a nonchalance that was rather upsetting.

"You angry?" he asked.

"I'm no king," Jaales replied. "I can see why you don't want him to succeed King Steffon. But . . ."

"You can't beat him. That it?" Delaquah kicked at a stone, as if they were passing the time in discussion of housing choices or first loves or inclement weather.

"I'm eager to live, yes." He put a hand on Delaquah's arm and turned toward him. "What's this about? I know you don't hate me, so what scheme do you have?"

"No scheme," he said, looking a bit affronted. "Listen carefully. You're every bit as strong as Mykol. And I'd take you in a match of endurance eight days in ten."

"That's reassuring."

"It's your choice of weapons and the nuances of their use that will put him off balance." Delaquah smiled wickedly.

"A hammer?" Jaales said incredulously.

"A hammer. A sword, too. He'll never have fought a man who filled his hands this way. He'll have no experience with it. While you," he gently poked Jaales's chest, "you've practiced against his so very unimaginative sword and shield. Practiced endlessly, I should say."

"Yes, I have *practiced*." He looked at Mykol, landing on his central question. "Is the contest one of submission? Or—"

Delaquah was shaking his head. "Victor's choice—"

"My dearest deafened gods, is this man a smithy?" It seemed Mykol had finally noticed Jaale's leather apron.

"He's a member of my company," Delaquah replied matter-of-factly. "Not surprising that it escaped you, what with his reds being soiled from honest work and all." The grin that spread on his captain's face was slim, but more perfectly incriminating for that.

59

Mykol's contempt at the suggestion of fighting a smith lasted all of two moments. It gave way to the man's practiced dismissiveness, as he turned his attention to Delaquah.

"Steffon would be ashamed of you. You may not respect me, but suggesting his replacement be a man whose best quality is shoeing a horse . . . You know I'll win. And you know it will be written that to earn the throne, I bested a simple blacksmith."

Jaale's had expected to see sharp anger in Delaquah's face. Maybe hear the man rip off a stream of curses and oaths. It wouldn't even have surprised him to see his captain take up his sword and sickle and challenge Mykol. But Delaquah did none of these things. He only smiled the smile of disappointment, and said, "You prove you have no vision. And the only throne such a man is fit for, is the one he must take to empty his bowels."

Mykol seemed to bite back a reply, his temples flexing as he clenched his teeth. Still staring at Delaquah, he spoke with the threat of mortal violence, "Have your man fill his hands."

Delaquah gave Jaales a reassuring pat on the lower back. "How will you fight?" he asked, his tone that of an expectant teacher, coaxing the correct answer from a student.

Jaales knew the answer: *With the Familiar.* But it didn't offer him any real comfort. "You've got him angry as a stirred hornet's nest. Thanks for that."

Delaquah turned his back to Mykol, so the other could neither see nor hear him speak. "He's a bit sloppy when his bile is up. That's not bad for you. Just don't rush. I doubt he's got a move different from anything you've seen a thousand times. On your side, minimum effort, my boy. Play catch to everything he throws. He's not weak, but you can outlast him."

"To become king?" Jaales said, mostly to himself.

Delaquah's brows rose. "Dear absent ones, is *that* your fear?"

"It's hard to imagine the path from hot iron to hot baths is a common one." Jaales then had what he hoped was an inspired notion. "If I win, can I select the replacement?"

Delaquah reached to Jaales belt and took hold of his new hammer, the one fashioned all of one material, and held it up between their faces. "What makes a king, then? The length of his sword? The place of his birth? The weight of his purse?" His captain spun the hammer like a top, stopped it. "Is it the number of men at his command? The number of men he's put down? The treaties he's signed, or refused to sign?"

"Obviously none of these," Jaales replied, growing tired of the mystery.

"Wrong."

"Then all of these."

"Wrong."

Jaales frowned, confused. "Do *you* even know?"

"Holy hells, boy, no. And neither does Mykol. And neither did Steffon before he took the bony seat. Are you starting to see?" Delaquah spun the hammer again.

"A king can come from anywhere," Jaales said, staring at his hammer.

"Half right," his captain said, adding an appropriate half smile. "What qualifies a man to be king is the willingness to do the job. And the commitment to try and do it well. Mykol wouldn't be a bad king, but he wouldn't be a good king, either. He's willing. I'll give him that. But I think he lacks something you've got, my boy."

Delaquah never said what that *something* was. He let it hang between them, like the hammer.

"You're more than a little crazy. You know that, right?" Jaales finally said.

His captain belted out a single blast of laughter. "Well then, clearly *I* should be king."

Jaales took hold of his hammer, drew his sword, and stepped past Delaquah toward the waiting heir apparent.

"One chance to submit. Do it now, and nothing is lost. You'll stay on as Delaquah's smithy." To his credit, Mykol's tone held no note of condescension.

Not trusting that any reply he'd make would sound right, Jaales simply shook his head.

Mykol's eyes shone with disapproval, but only for a moment before he came at him. Came hard. The clangor of steel against the solid iron of Jaales's hammer rang out around them. Then again, and again.

Jaales gave ground, being pushed back into the trees, but not in a panic. He methodically deflected or blocked or evaded each strike, not yet attempting to counterstrike. The whole thing seemed eerily like his training sessions with Delaquah. He fell into familiar patterns, his skin becoming hot and slick with the work of it.

Mykol pushed harder, his irritation clear. And Jaales gave more ground, careful as he moved rearward down a well trodden path. And into the small clearing where he worked his trade.

A thin smile flickered on the other man's face as they pushed through into the work yard. Jaales guessed the captain found some poetic irony in the thought of killing Jaales here, among his tools and coals.

But if anything, Jaales thought the fight coming here was to his advantage. The familiarity.

Then Mykol stood back, panting lightly. He sidled up to a weapons rack, tossed aside his shield, and picked up a spear. It was a fighting technique Jaales hadn't trained against. Well, not more than a handful of times, anyway.

Is it time to stop defending? Go at him?

The would-be king gave him no time to decide, launching forward. The spear came in fast. Jaales parried it away with his sword, and brought his hammer down in a short, powerful arc. He caught the man in the upper chest, folding a deep dent in his breastplate. The blow rang soundly, and sent Mykol flailing back three steps.

But he came at him again. This time, the man feigned throwing the spear. Jaales swung his sword, anticipating the spear, and lost his balance when he realized Mykol hadn't let the weapon fly. The next thing he felt was the sharp pain of metal piercing his flesh. The spear went deep, into his upper chest below his collar bone. The blow drove him back, and he fell hard into the tools and racks of his own forge.

Mykol had gone down on his knees, but recovered, and scurried toward him with his sword.

Jaales couldn't lift his left arm. The pain was too excruciating. He could try to fend off an attack with his good arm and his hammer. But for how long?

His eyes were clouding. Was he losing blood? Losing consciousness?

He then realized he was staring up at Mykol through a thin skein of quicklime that had puffed up when he'd sailed into his forger's table. He looked around and found the overturned bucket.

Fight with the familiar.

When Mykol reared back to deal a heavy blow, Jaales feigned paralysis, staring wide-eyed up at his attacker. Until the last moment. Then he rolled out of the way, and threw a handful of quicklime directly into the man's eyes.

The captain screamed in pain. He dropped his sword and tried to clear his eyes with trembling hands. His tears were already streaking tracks through his powdered face. Then he scrambled backward, knowing he was defenseless. Perhaps he hoped to regain his sight and find a weapon strewn about from one of the fallen racks.

But the quicklime wouldn't stop burning for a good long time. Only Jaales knew this. He pushed himself to his feet, his left arm dangling, and walked slowly in pursuit.

His mind churned. *How do I end this?*

As he neared Mykol, who remained unable to open his eyes, Jaales noticed the hundreds of men surrounding his little workshop. Men in neatly pressed red. Men in soiled red. Delaquah, with an expression Jaales hadn't anticipated. A kind of sad frown. But with no instruction for him.

Finally, Mykol stopped scrambling away. He'd not gone in a direction where he'd find a weapon. He seemed now to know that. Just as he also seemed resigned to the fact that he'd not regain his sight in time to be of any help to himself.

Jaales lifted his hammer, considering. The realization of what had just happened began to fall on him like a heavy yoke.

In the silence, Mykol spoke. "I would have killed you. You should do the same." The profession wasn't bitter, or defeated, or challenging. It was just a profession.

Jaales looked up again at the two companies, men waiting to see what he'd do. Beyond them, beyond the trees, sat his war engines, waiting for them to finish a siege. Waiting for them to reclaim a city and any of its people that were still alive.

Jaales dropped his hammer suggestively close to Mykol's head, then rushed to gather a pale of water. When he returned, he knelt beside the man and began irrigating his eyes.

"You might lose the use of them. But we might save some of your sight." He kept at it, dipping a hand towel into the bucket and squeezing out the water into the corners of the man's eyes, flushing the chemical away.

"I would have killed you," Mykol said again. This time, the sound of the words came limned with shame.

"Then I would have been dead," Jaales said rather perfunctorily.

As he continued to work at the man's eyes, Delaquah sauntered forward, a healthy bit of "I told you so" in his swagger. "You're always a surprise, my boy." He paused, stroking his beard. "But ah, we don't have the luxury of time, do we." He smiled broadly. "What does the king command?"

Jaales didn't have to think long. "As soon as we're done here, we'll finish what we started. Take back Graas."

He returned his attention to Mykol's ruined eyes. "Before you put on the lion red, what did you do? What were you good at?"

The man did not immediately reply. Some hesitance, Jaales thought. "My lord, I wrote songs for my parents' inn."

Jaales smiled. He was glad the man couldn't see it, since he would have misinterpreted the expression.

"But I'm deft with strategy, my lord," Mykol hastened to add. "Field position and timing and the right compliment of men and engines."

Jaales heard Delaquah over his shoulder. "I hate to admit it, but that's the truth."

Jaales soaked the rag again, squeezing more water into the man's burning eyes. "Then you'll remain in my counsel. And I'll want your best songs, besides. To commemorate those who fall. That suit you?"

"My lord," the man said, his voice humble with gratitude.

"That all?" Delaquah asked.

Jaales considered. No that was not all. "Our three fastest riders will return to Ir-Caul. And from there, messengers into every town and city in Alon I'tol." He smiled at his own thoughts. "Bright hells, send them into Kamas, Vohnce, Wynstout, Divad. Any smith willing to work for us, we'll give him triple his pay. Blacksmiths, white-smiths, carpenters, men good with glass and gears and engines."

Delaquah was nodding with enthusiasm, his face bright with understanding. "Damn fine plan."

SACRIFICE

OF THE

FIRST SHEASON

INTRODUCTION

I SPENT A LONG TIME in world creation for The Vault of Heaven. I remember sitting on my apartment floor for months writing up events, places, peoples. I drew maps. I wrote vignettes. I dreamed. Some were violent dreams. But who's keeping score?

An important sequence in all that world development was the founding of the world. Gods and councils. Charters and principles. And all the ways it could turn south. Go wrong. The moments that set big conflicts in motion. Things to lie dormant for ages.

So, as I started to write these tales along the way—to share some of those moments of the long past— this story came first.

It frames some of what I find important about the idea of service. Of putting others first.

In that regard, watch for Efram. There's more about him in *Trial of Intentions*. I love the hell out of him. I kind of wish our world had more Eframs. I'd sleep a lot better if it did.

Sacrifice
of the First Sheason

DEEP IN THE **D**IVIDE Mountains, wind and thunder shook
conifers that towered a hundred strides tall. Rain fell hard,
battering the village of Estem Salo and leaving it awash in the sound
of rushing waters. Lightning struck every few moments, flashing
the world beyond Palamon Dal Solaas' window in stark, momentary relief before darkness reclaimed the heights around his home.
Beside him, Solera slept soundly, nestled into the crook of his arm.
But *he* could not sleep, finding the tempest in the heavens too disquieting. So, when Palamon first heard the pounding at his door
over the tumult of the storm, he had a sense of foreboding about
the late night caller. *Who would brave these storms at this hour?*

The heavy beating at his door came again, faster this time, more
insistent. Quickly but carefully he freed his arm from beneath his
slumbering companion and hurried to the door. He could imagine
only a member of the council coming to him at this hour. He'd seen
them in private chambers often lately; perhaps this visit was related to
these new secrets. His visitor would likely be Dossolum, the Voice
of the Council, who'd been struggling to maintain balance as the
Founders labored to complete their formation of this world.

71

When Palamon pulled open his door, he looked instead into the dripping, strained face of his fellow Sheason, Manoa.

"Palamon, please, will you come with me? There's trouble and I need help." Manoa ran a hand over his face in a futile attempt to wipe off the rain, which struck his cheeks and forehead in torrents.

Palamon did not hesitate. As he pulled on a heavy greatcloak and slipped into high boots set beside his door, he asked, "What is the problem?"

"There's a disturbance of some kind in the town of Melas Tal. They've sent for me as intercessor." Manoa stood back and pointed an arm weighted by his own sodden cloak toward a figure in shadow sitting astride a horse. "This man will show us the way."

"You usually don't ask for help, my friend," Palamon said. "What is this disturbance?"

Just then Solera came into the room, bearing a hand lamp that dimly lit the walls around them. "What is it, Palamon?" she asked.

Manoa explained. "This man's wife," he said, still indicating the shadowed man waiting several paces back in the night, "there are complications with the birth of her child. I would tend to her, but there is trouble elsewhere in Melas Tal. Palamon. Please, we must go."

The other Sheason looked back at his companion. "I will be back as quickly as I can."

Solera nodded, and came close to give him a brief kiss. She then shut the door behind him as he ran to his mount, which Manoa already had waiting for him. The other man came into dim view as Palamon climbed into his saddle. His eyes looked haunted, his face drawn with sleeplessness and worry. His great beard did not move when he offered a "thank you" Palamon could barely hear over the sound of the downpour.

The bearded man led them into the night. Palamon focused on the dark trail, working to keep pace with the man, whom Manoa called Efram. They slowed several times, but only to rest the horses before pushing hard again through the night and the storm. Three hours they rode before coming upon the town. Manoa bade them farewell, then veered sharply to the north on his own errand.

Palamon continued to follow Efram, and shortly they were pulling up beside a low cottage that seemed to hunker close to the earth in the darkness. They dismounted fast, and the man got the door open as Palamon rushed inside.

What he saw nearly stopped his heart.

In a simple home, adorned with hand-hewn chairs and uneven pots and thick shawls knitted of dull brown yarn, a young girl, maybe six years old, sat at the foot of her mother's bed holding an infant that did not cry or stir. Palamon kept moving, his own boots loud in his ears as he neared the child. Closer, he could see a bluish hue to the babe's skin. At that moment, Efram swept past him and landed hard on his knees in front of his daughter, who began to weep as her father wrapped both her and her dead baby brother in a grief-stricken embrace.

"I didn't know what to do," the little girl said through her sobs. "I tried and tried, but he stopped breathing. Mama is too sick. There was no one else to help . . ."

Efram brushed tears from his daughter's cheeks and gently took the babe from her arms. He looked down at the child's face with a profound sadness Palamon would never forget. Then the man tenderly pulled the blanket swaddling the babe around to cover its face, and gently laid it in a nearby crib fashioned of whittled pine boughs sitting at the foot of the bed.

After a moment there, the man knelt at his wife's side and stroked her forehead to rouse her. "Volleia," he whispered. "Volleia, I've brought help."

The woman's eyes fluttered open. "My child."

Efram lied. "The baby is fine, dear one, no need to bother with that. But you, how are you?"

Volleia never replied, her eyes closing again. Efram pulled back the covers and showed Palamon.

"She's lost a lot of blood, Sheason. Too much. And she still bleeds." The man turned around, still on his knees, and took Palamon's hand in his own rough-skinned palms. "I beg you, don't let her die."

Efram's voice remained steady, but came so softly that Palamon almost could not hear it. "I came too late to save my son; don't let me lose my dear one, too."

Palamon then sensed another presence and turned to see the young girl likewise kneeling before him. She reached up with her small hand and put it over her father's.

As Sheason, he had studied healing arts, and might be able to help, but there was no guarantee. And their supplication made him uncomfortable besides. He lifted their hands, urging them to their feet, and away from the bed.

He sat at the woman's side and leaned close, and gently placed a hand on her chest. She stirred, and opened her eyes. She looked up at him, staring first at the Sheason pendant hanging around his neck, then up into his face.

After a moment, silent tears began to fall from the corners of her eyes. "My child is dead. I can see it in your face," Volleia whispered. She swallowed hard. "Can you not save my son?" she asked.

Palamon could hear his own breath, hear the creak of the bed and floorboards and the burn of the lamp. He heard the howl of the storm beyond the cottage walls, and thought he could hear the strained cry of a newborn in the wind that shrilled around the eaves. In that moment, he felt a kind of grief he had not ever felt.

He looked back at the pleading mother and said as tenderly as he could, "My good woman, it is not given to me to breathe life back into a form that has gone to its earth. But I ask you not to despair. These loved ones behind me need you, and it will take all our combined strength to make you well."

But she did not hear most of his words. Even now she slipped toward death. Perhaps the realization that her babe could not be saved was too much to bear, and so she yielded to death's embrace. Or maybe she was fighting to stay alive. Regardless, Palamon knew he faced a mighty challenge. Her life energy was fading fast, and despite all he could do, she might yet pass this life and leave her family behind.

Palamon lowered his head and began to utter words in the conceiver tongue. He drew out healing herbs and pried open her mouth, crumbling them onto her tongue. He had cold water brought, and wiped the woman down to reduce her fever, likewise cleansing her body of the blood and applying a salve to the damage in her womanhood to stop further bleeding. He hadn't the power to render the Will to heal her, but his quiet words seemed to impart the stillness of peace as best he could to her battered mother's soul.

For hours he worked, constantly cooling her skin with a wet rag, administering further doses of herb, speaking words of comfort and hope though she remained unconscious. Near on to morning, his strength flagged, having offered so much of himself that he began to swoon. He braced himself with one arm and kept on. At last, his own eyes closed and he felt himself falling from exhaustion.

WHEN MANOA ROUSED HIM he did not know how long he'd been sleeping.

"Palamon."

On his lips, Palamon tasted the mint of the Cloudwood sprig the Sheason harvested and used for renewal. No doubt his friend had placed it on Palamon's tongue while he slept.

"She is well?" Palamon asked, feeling some certainty about it, and sat up.

In reply, Manoa stood back, allowing Efram to come forward. Palamon saw grief in the man's eyes, but strangely he thought he saw gratitude, too. The man said nothing, only looking at Palamon, his eyes never once showing tears. Rather, again his rough hands took hold of Palamon's own, and he squeezed with a might that suggested great strength and the acknowledgment of a debt.

The young girl stepped up beside her father and offered a much-loved doll as if in payment—a gesture Palamon could tell required great sacrifice on her part. He smiled weakly, and handed the toy back to the child. "Keep her safe for me," he said. The girl hugged the doll close to her cheek.

Manoa then assisted Palamon to his feet. It was then that he saw the woman lying under a sheet on the bed, her face covered over.

She was dead.

"I'm sorry," Palamon offered. "I tried . . ."

Efram nodded.

Then Manoa helped him out of the cottage and onto his mount. Together, he and the intercessor for the people of this new world rode away as slowly and lazily as the smoke that streamed from Efram's fieldstone chimney.

The sun broke over the mountains to the east, the storm clouds gone from the skies. Palamon thought to ask his Sheason friend what disturbance he'd seen to while Palamon had tried to save a family. But he forgot his question beneath the searing mental images of the young girl holding the dead child, the woman he'd tried to save but could not, and the receding visage of Efram, who watched them from his doorstep until the road wound out of sight of the man's humble home.

CAS&O

SEVERAL DAYS LATER, Palamon stood at the foot of the tabernacle steps and frowned. Blood from the body on the marble steps above had pooled in the soft loam near his feet. The figure had been brutalized to a point where he could tell only that it had once been a man. But one thing was clear: this was no accident

The savagery of the attack, all too evident, sickened him. He looked up, as he always did when he needed to gather himself. Against the bright blue heavens, the great pillars of the Tabernacle of the Sky rose like sentinels guarding the sacred place that had witnessed the founding of the world. It stood in majesty, unassailable, beautiful, almost as if its heights held up the sky itself. And here, high in the mountains of the Divide, the sky seemed already a close thing.

Palamon took a deep, bracing breath of cool early morning air. Before this, there had not been bloodshed. Not in this world. There'd been death of the natural kind, mishap or disease or the struggle of childbirth—he knew those only too well. But *this* kind of death was not supposed to come until later, in due course, when *intentional* travail beset the races the Founders, who strode the halls of the tabernacle, had fashioned to populate the land.

It should not have begun so soon.

Not . . . *deliberately.*

Palamon, first servant among the Sheason whom the Great Ones had created first to aid them, steeled himself to look back down at the broken body. Seeing it again, he thought he could now smell the iron in the drying blood. And though perhaps only in his mind, he thought he saw an expression of confusion and fear still resting in the man's purpled cheeks. Whoever this had been had not expected such violence —nor would he have had cause to. Not yet.

The position of the body told another story.

This still-unnamed world—more vast than most the Fathers had created for eons—was in its infancy. Its wide geography stood yet mostly vacant of inhabitants. The exodus into the wildernesses that existed far from the tabernacle had only just begun. Still, none of those created by the Fathers ever came *here.* In the land below the mountains of the Tabernacle they lived and tilled and settled. The tabernacle itself would have been unknown to them, or if some-how known, unthinkable to approach.

Whatever had slain this man had unique knowledge of this place and meant to leave the crushed heap of flesh as a message. In its desecration of the tabernacle . . . it was a warning; its presence a dire harbinger.

But from whom? Who would threaten the Council of the Gods by raining down blood on the steps to this sacred place? In this high season of creation, even those beings made deliberately to harrow the lives of men hadn't yet such rancor or temerity. *Or has something changed?*

Surveying the wreckage of flesh and the red runnels of blood now stiff from hours of exposure to chill air, Palamon felt a shiver deep in his soul. Something in the founding of this world had gone wrong. He looked back up past the heights of the tabernacle toward the open, wind-swept sky, but could not reclaim his sense of peace. Some taint had gotten into the very fabric of things. He could feel it.

Perhaps it was because he worked so closely with Dossolum, the Voice of the Council, that he sensed such things. The long periods he'd spent together with Dossolum in consultation, recording what had been done, what lay ahead, retrieving archived information carried forward from other worlds ... all of it endowed Palamon with an understanding none of the other Sheason possessed. Dossolum trusted him more than the other Founders did their attendants, helping Palamon to gain—over years of counsel and attentive service—an acute intuition.

As he slowly climbed toward the battered body, something came into terrible focus. He shook his head as he knelt beside the lifeless form and gingerly pulled it over onto its back. Grief and fear struck him when he saw that the dead man was Manoa. Not a man created by the Fathers to live in this world, but a Sheason, like Palamon himself . . .

In this fledgling place, Manoa had held a special stewardship: to guide and teach. He'd worn the mantle of intercessor with the Great Ones on behalf of men, for those times when the work at the Founders' hands might prove imbalanced.

If laying a torn and bloodied body on the steps of the tabernacle had been a message, this was a challenge. Or worse. It showed utter disregard for the tabernacle and those who walked its vaulted halls. Could there have been something more ancient, something more malevolent residing in the very matter they'd used to create this youngest of worlds?

Staring into one of Manoa's empty eye-sockets, Palamon thought it could be nothing as remarkable as that. Rather, as he recalled the gentleness of this servant, how the man had delighted in the companionship of others; how he had struggled—but persisted—with his own efforts at song, and laughed to make others feel comfortable when argument over the work grew heated, Palamon's suspicions grew. He became convinced that whatever—whoever—was to blame had been specifically aware of the significance of *this* death, this *Sheason*.

And so, sitting at the foot of creation, next to the tortured body of a gentle man, he grieved. But in his heart he felt also the stirrings of wrath—an anger that had as yet no target.

Sometime later, stirred from grief and anger by the shrill cry of a mountain raptor, Palamon stood and gently picked up his dead friend's body and carried it into a stand of towering hemlocks. Just before easing the body into its final earth he shifted the body so that he could gently lay it down. As he put his hand under Manoa's neck to guide him into his grace, his hand caught on something hard and sharp, drawing blood. He pulled from Manoa's garment a serrated tooth half the length of his finger, studied it a moment, and dropped it into his pocket. He then finished digging the grave and burying his friend within sight of the tabernacle—Manoa would have liked that. Then he returned and washed away the blood from the steps before others came to the tabernacle to resume their labors of creation.

CB&O

PALAMON RODE HARD to Estem Salo, some ten leagues from the tabernacle. The small town sat in a high valley of the Divide surrounded by forests of white pine and aspen. He kicked his horse often, riding directly to the archives where the Sheason did most of their work. Even before his mount had stopped, he leapt to the ground and rushed through the door into the warm light of oil lamps and the scent of burning candles. Usually these things calmed him and set the tenor of his studies. Today, his heart raced with urgency to find one person and one piece of information.

On the main floor he dashed around study tables and shelves of books and working Sheason, angling toward the left wall, and Solera.

Let her be here.

His wife would ordinarily be recording those things spoken at the tabernacle the evening before. These days she was responsible for documenting the many species and the uniqueness of each. She would record the gifts inherent in the formation of life, and those instilled by the framers. It was a delicate and difficult task, since the strengths and weaknesses of each species had to be balanced with those of all the others. The Fathers had taken this all into account, but the nuances of their creations were not easy to articulate. And increasingly, those who walked the Sky relied on Solera to inform their labors in advance. Her gift in this regard was matchless.

But the burden of it—writing and informing the harmony they all sought for the people now being set upon the land—often took her out of the archive to rest her mind. Most often, she went to their aspen grove, where the slightest stirring of the wind brought the sound of rippling leaves that she described as laughter.

He hoped she had not gone there today. As he slammed into the study where she worked, he realized that for the first time he was feeling mortal dread.

But immediately upon entering he saw her. She held a stylus in one hand. And when she looked up, an expression of surprise turned fast to irritation. As she started to scold him for being so careless and interrupting her, he drew her up from her seat and pulled her close.

He felt her finally return his embrace. "What is wrong?" she asked.

Palamon hugged her tighter still. The thoughts that had run through his mind . . . he couldn't imagine life without her. She was his greatest happiness: sharing their evenings, making love, exploring topics that, despite their work with the Founders, continued to elude him and Solera both.

She drew back and repeated, "What is wrong?"

Briefly, Palamon considered telling her all he knew. And more than that, all he feared. The death of Manoa, the placement of the body, the bit of sharp bone in his pocket, and a few rumors he now recalled about one member of the council he'd not allowed himself to think too much upon . . . all of it led his mind to conclusions he hoped yet might prove false.

"Nothing," he finally said. "Just some foolishness. I'm sorry. Go back to your work."

He tried to leave, but she grabbed his hand with firm insistence. "Not good enough. If you want to tell me that you're in a rush, and that you'll explain later, I can accept that. And only if there's nothing I can do to help. But don't play false with your need and emotions. Or mine."

Still feeling the urgency of his second reason for hurrying to the Archive, he nevertheless smiled. "I love that you keep me honest. But it isn't something I would speak of here." Palamon looked over his shoulder. "I don't want to worry anyone until I have answers."

"And you don't need my help," she said, her brows rising to suggest her offer to assist.

"Not yet." Palamon squeezed her fingers in reassurance. He then quickly took his leave, pulling the door shut again, much harder than he'd intended. But he was already rushing to the stairs. He paid no mind to either greetings or looks of concern and surprise as he sped past other Sheason engaged in their work.

Up three flights of stairs he raced, glancing at many who sat at tables and carefully recorded in books and ledgers. He dashed past others who stood near smoothly plastered walls. Upon these walls were philosophies and precise drawings pertaining to those words, and all setting forth the guiding principles spoken by the Framers in the Tabernacle of the Sky.

A few called after him, inquiring, and one—Ilana—scolding. He ignored them all. Then he reached the fourth floor and wound his way recklessly between reading and study tables to a rear room with a closed door. He pulled up short, breathing hard. He clenched his teeth, firmly pressed on the latch, and threw open the door.

He desperately wanted a confrontation, but there would be none. The room lay empty. Still, what he needed to find was here. *It must be!* Palamon rushed to low shelves and long, wide drawers, rifling through sheaves of parchment and strange, dark papyrus written on with a silver ink.

He found nothing, and so forced himself to stop and think of his next course of action. The Sheason who served Maldea, the member of the council set apart to refine mankind by challenging it with adversity, would have a filing system. Palamon had never been in this room to study or record, and knew he wasn't supposed to be here even now. But he had to find out what was really going on. It stood to reason that Maldea's Sheason would keep organized records.

Palamon took the bit of bone from his pocket and looked at it more closely. He noticed now that blood—it had to be Manoa's blood—had dried in the serrated grooves. A fresh surge of loss and anger swept through him, lending him a savage calm. He went back to the shelves and focused his search. A few minutes later, what he found left him feeling the kind of despair he'd thought he might never feel.

The Sheason who served Maldea had distilled their labors into elegant classifications and formulas that could easily and incrementally be added to the work Palamon and his brothers and sisters had been doing to aid the council. In the simple life of a flower or blossoming bush or high-growth tree, in the quality of sunlight, hue of water, and richness of the soil, in the forms of animal life, these servants had in most cases made only the subtlest change to poison or sully the purpose of that which the Founders had set forth on the land. It was genius. It was an abomination.

With only a fraction of the effort, they'd produced a set of formation principles that would undo so much of what had been done since the dawn of this world's creation.

And then, they had begun their real work.

Palamon moved fast, consuming what he could of the plans prepared by Maldea and those who served him. His throat tightened as he read; the room seemed to grow hot.

He could feel his own mind pricked with a canker at the simple introduction of these thoughts and semantics. He'd seen none of these things in the world beyond the archive, and yet here it was, written in the dark pages of this quiet study.

He looked up, needing a break. Learning of these malefic things had strained him to the point of panting. His chest felt constricted. His hands were quivering as he went to the single window and pushed it open to gasp some air. Slowly, he regained the rhythms of his own heart and breathing, and hunkered down before a last bookcase. He ran his fingers over the spines, the intuition he had honed in so many years as Dossolum's right arm warning him vaguely about what he would find.

Then his fingers stopped, and he drew forth a volume with one hand, squeezing the bony tooth with his other, feeling neither its bite nor the blood that trickled through his clenched fist.

He thumbed open the tome, reading its title scrawled in long pen-strokes: *Y'Tilat Mor Sonctal Fanumen*. Palamon dropped the book, and his hands again began to shake. He dared not think or utter the meaning of these words, written in the language of dominion and conception used by the First Ones themselves to call forth the world.

Here, sitting on a simple corner bookshelf in Esteem Salo, this book spoke of *that which went beyond.*

But Palamon remembered his friend Manoa, who'd been cast upon the marble steps of the Tabernacle of the Sky, and steadied his nerves once more. He began to turn back the pages, learning things that only the gods themselves should know and looking at the renderings of an expert hand. These illustrations showed creatures that people in their darkest nightmares could not have seen.

Again, Palamon despaired. But he did not stop.

He read onward, taking in the images drawn on the pages and the words that accompanied them, powerful verse crafted in a tongue that Palamon himself had never been allowed to fully know, even as close as he was to Dossolum.

Then he paused. His hand no longer trembled as he stared at the page and the image of a creation—no, a demon that defied description, except for its open, snarling maw that exposed rows and rows . . . of serrated teeth.

In his mind, Palamon suddenly played grisly scenarios of the death of his friend, who had had no notion of hatred.

And Palamon realized, as he saw it in his mind, that so much of what he'd seen this day might only be prelude to what may come. Bloodshed was inevitable (and even necessary), but only after the High Season, after creation was complete; until then the Founders' will and benevolence (at least from what Palamon had read of other worlds) held sway in the hearts of men. Here, the land had been formed, the light of the heavens by day and night prepared, the vegetation and animals placed, man most recently . . . but this kind of treachery should not yet have been unleashed into *this* world.

What he had seen in the book had flowed from a diseased mind, and Palamon had to let Dossolum know. The very intention of the council, all their work, was at risk. Still reading, he stood.

"You're not allowed in here," a voice said.

Startled, Palamon whirled. Jo'ha'nel, Maldea's primary Sheason, towered in the doorway. His wide shoulders supported a thin, almost emaciated torso, but he gave the feeling of coiled power. He was attired all in black, tight-fitting clothes. His breeches were lashed to his legs with dark leather strips that wound up from his boots to his knees. Dark, silken hair fell down around his pale face.

"Manoa has been killed," Palamon said. "I fear something wrought by Maldea's hand is the cause."

"Be careful of your accusations, brother." Jo'ha'nel smiled.

Palamon found renewed calm at the thought of the work taking place in the outer rooms. They were not alone. He stared back. "Deny it."

The other laughed. "I am not yours to question, Palamon. Founders are not supposed to esteem one Sheason over another, and regardless, Dossolum's fondness for you doesn't worry me."

"I do not ask for him," Palamon said. "I ask for the fallen."

Jo'ha'nel did not reply, but instead turned in the doorway and cast his gaze back into the archive where Sheason worked diligently at their many tasks. "Look at them," he said. "Enamored of their own books and philosophies. You know, of course, that Dossolum has even asked them now to fashion a system of beliefs, morality . . . religion for your weaker races."

"Why do you say *yours*, Jo'ha'nel? The work belongs to *all* of us. We are not at odds, you and I. I help in bringing life to this place. Your part is to assist in that which will provide challenge and trial to the people of this world, so that they might find within themselves their own greatness."

"You are naive," the other said, and laughed.

"Then you do not deny that it is your craft that gave rise to this." He thrust the open book toward Jo'ha'nel like an indictment, showing him the page where the creature was drawn.

The other would not be baited. "Let us follow your reason, shall we? If the role of Maldea and we who serve him is to create that which will burden and test those that flow from your merciful bowels, then this," he pointed at the book, "represents nothing more than our desire for mankind to achieve his utmost." Again he flashed the dark smile.

"You exaggerate your role, Jo'ha'nel. This world is in a delicate balance just now. We are at only the beginning of imparting to the people the values that will lead them to the ethics of the Charter."

Maldea's primary Sheason frowned at the mention of this last. He muttered to himself, "Charter." Then he turned in the doorway, squaring his wide shoulders and willowy frame toward Palamon. "The Charter is a fool's doctrine. Its adherents will fall when greed and gluttony and pride fill the hearts of men."

"Your mind is twisted," Palamon countered. "These are the very things the Charter is written to safeguard against. Without it, this world—any world—would crumble beneath the weight of its inhabitants' baser instincts."

"And why base, Palamon? Because Dossolum says it is so?" Jo'ha'nel glared at him.

As Palamon returned the stare, he realized something. "You knew. You knew Manoa was going to be killed and you did nothing." And on the heels of this knowledge came something more. "And Manoa is not the only one, is he?"

The other's lips pulled back into an unsmiling grin that revealed carious teeth—Jo'ha'nel was changing . . .

"You will not succeed," Palamon said softly but with defiance. "I won't allow it."

"*You* won't allow it." At that, Jo'ha'nel threw his head back and laughed. The hoarse sound of it was like the tearing of parchment. "You are a scholar, a historian, and maybe—at the best of times—a sage. But you lack any *power* to stem this tide, Palamon. Not even the one you serve can turn it back."

At that instant, Jo'ha'nel raised an upturned palm and pulled his fingers back in a summoning gesture. The book Palamon held was ripped from his hands and flew into the clutches of Maldea's Sheason.

Dear Sky, he's been given the power to render the Will!

Feeling helpless and exposed, Palamon yet held his ground, and looked back intently. "Don't do this, Jo'ha'nel. You know why we came here. Don't let this new gospel confuse you." He pointed at the book the other now held tight to his chest. "Think on what it has done. This fiend has taken life. He's ended all that Manoa was or could ever be. It puts the essence of things, matter and spirit— Forda I'Forza—out of balance."

"No!" the other cried. "There you are wrong. Balance remains. The difference is only who, on this world, will define that balance

. . . and how. We are simply rewriting what your scribblers so arrogantly and ignorantly pen at the behest of the council." Jo'ha'nel pointed behind him at the archive study tables.

Palamon shook his head. This was madness. He looked it in the face. Jo'ha'nel, once his brother, now glared at him with malefic eyes. This servant's countenance had changed in a way that left Palamon feeling cold for both the loss of a friend and the baneful intention he could see there.

"You are wise, Palamon. You need to consider on which side you will stand when the time comes."

Then Jo'ha'nel raised a hand and quietly spoke a few words; a faint light pulsed across all the drawers and shelves of the dark study. *He's sealing the books.*

With that Jo'ha'nel tucked under his arm the book he still held and slowly walked to the stairs without looking back.

Palamon surveyed the room, wondering what other dark arts were hidden in the writings around him. He could now feel the taint of this corner study, and hastened to leave. Once he got out of Jo'ha'nel's room, his breathing eased and his mind cleared. With that, a single question occurred to him, and he rushed after the dark Sheason—once his friend—intent on having the answer. All the way to the door on the main level he ran, then into the street. But Jo'ha'nel had disappeared.

And like salt poured into a wound, even as he stood there panting, peering down the street, rumors began to arrive, riders, messenger birds, all bearing the same news: the blood of innocents was drenching the land. And often the deaths reported were not quick, but savage and punishing.

ᏣᎦᏍᎤ

A FEW DAYS LATER Dossolum arrived in the Sheason village and gave Palamon a grave look; without a word they turned east, each knowing the other's mind. They trod the path as they did once every cycle of the Lesser Light. From Estem Salo, they walked in silence all the way to the edge of a great promontory.

Now, Palamon stood at the precipice. Beside him, still unspeaking, was Dossolum. Through the hazy light of early evening, they looked far away to the south and east. On the horizon slightly to their left some few stars had winked into life with the imminent arrival of night. Up from the face of the cliff rose a warm, gentle breeze scented with juniper and oak. It gusted lightly every few moments, causing the whisper of leaves as they fluttered in the wind.

Palamon looked up into the half moon and smiled wanly. He was thinking of the peace, now lost, that he'd so recently known when gazing upon its simple beauty. It hung low in the dimming azure sky.

After a time, Dossolum's deep, resonant voice broke the silence between them. "You have secrets, my friend."

Palamon's smile faded. "That you ask tells me they are not secrets."

"And yet you did not choose to discuss them with me. Why?"

"I have no answers for my questions, no solutions to the problems I've encountered," Palamon replied. "I hoped to bring you more than the trouble itself. The killings are only part of the story. I believe we can yet rescue Jo'ha'nel."

It was Dossolum's turn to smile. "You've a good heart, Palamon. But at times it makes you unwise." The Voice of the Council raised a hand toward the expanse before them, where far away and below a few small villages and one sizable town could be seen on the horizon. "Should we suffer more of these mortals to die while we seek answers to one Sheason's sickness?"

"I ask your forgiveness," Palamon said, offering a slight bow. "I thought I could find an answer quickly. Surely it's been written of . . . occurred before."

Dossolum shifted his stance and looked at him. "There has been arrogance and pretense, yes. And there have been challenges in the formation of many worlds. Even bloodshed like Manoa's."

"I've not seen these records in the Archives," Palamon said. "Wouldn't those help us find answers to what is happening now?"

"We've not recorded these, because it is not a pattern we wish to repeat." Dossolum's countenance drew taut with a faraway look, as if in remembrance. "There've been worlds, my friend, where our efforts have not gone precisely as we might have hoped. The temptations of Maldea's office—to create all that is baneful; in particular, creatures that revel in violence against all other creations—these temptations are strong. Other council members who have held that office in the formation of other worlds have nearly gone too far . . ."

Palamon shivered. He'd not heard Dossolum speak of such things. Even the tone of his voice had changed, sounding doubtful and sad.

The Voice of the Council then turned to look at him. "But never," he said, giving Palamon a regretful look, "never to this degree. This is the dawning of a new corruption, a new sorrow … a new damnation. I ask you to waste no more time in seeking a cure. We will have enough to do just annulling this awful work."

Palamon's intuition revealed a terrifying suggestion in Dossolum's words. He turned to look at the Voice of the Council. "What would you ask of me?"

Dossolum smiled. "You are a serious man, my friend. I suspect it is why I've taken you to my right. But you've become more than a helpmate; I have never had so good a friend as you."

"Thank you. And I am not always so serious," Palamon said, smiling at his own denial.

"No, not always," Dossolum conceded. "But you have a keen mind. You are first among your Sheason brothers not because you stand at my right, but rather you stand there *because* of that mind of yours."

Palamon turned and looked back at the horizon. This promontory, which he'd come to consider sacred, looked out over lands that stretched for leagues east of the Divide Mountains. Countless times he and Dossolum had stood right here, taking in the view, considering the work in which they were engaged. And now, the work itself had ground to a halt under suspicions and the chaos of so much violent death.

Finally, he only nodded to Dossolum's words. When the Founder spoke, there was hardly any opinion in it; he was a truth speaker, the Voice of the Council.

Another companionable silence fell between them, as each considered, Palamon guessed, his own grave thoughts. Dossolum later placed a hand on Palamon's shoulder, preparatory to speaking again.

"They will not survive," he said.

Surprise and panic filled Palamon. "Nonsense. The council will surely put a stop to Maldea's efforts. And Jo'ha'nel will fall in line once that is done."

"And what of the vile species given life by Maldea's hand? What of them?"

Palamon considered the words, and said again, "What would you ask of me?"

Silence stretched for long moments before Dossolum spoke. "Palamon, I am going to confer upon you the authority to render the Will and the office of intercessor for the people of this world."

Dossolum's hand on his shoulder suddenly felt very heavy. He could only think that this responsibility came as a result of recent changes, in Maldea and Jo'ha'nel—and because of the death of his friend. He feared that he would have to use this new authority not —as it was intended—to create and sustain, but to defend . . . and destroy.

"Jo'ha'nel has been given the power of the Will," Palamon said. "He wields it, I fear, with ill-intent. And with Manoa dead, someone must answer this threat," Palamon deduced, with some bitterness.

Dossolum surprised him when he said simply, "Yes." Then after several moments he added, "But not only that, Palamon. You have been on this path for a long time. Have you not already been among the people, providing comfort?"

Looking out over the wide terrain, Palamon nodded and thought of Efram and his little girl . . . and the woman and child he'd been too late to save.

Dossolum made a sound deep in his throat. "They will not survive unless there is one to protect them."

"With more than a quill and his knowledge of history, you mean," Palamon said, and offered a faltering smile. "You see, I am not always so serious."

Dossolum returned the smile. "Kneel, my friend."

Palamon knelt, steadying himself with his hands on the ground and feeling the cool earth beneath his fingers. He closed his eyes as the Voice of the Council began to speak in a commanding yet soothing tone.

"As it lives in me, so shall it live in you, Palamon Dal Solaas. The right and privilege to stir and direct the Will that resides in all things, in all Forda I'Forza, I give you. It is a gift and power to be used wisely, never selfishly, and never to bring harm to the lives of mortals. With this authority you may direct and shape the things around you, even unto the healing of that which is broken, body or spirit. You have proven worthy of this endowment, Palamon; generations will revere you, peace will be yours, and the world may have hope now as you take the mantle of intercessor for the people of an imperiled world."

Dossolum's hand never left Palamon's shoulder, and in the moments that followed, his entire body warmed from within. His mind filled with hopeful thoughts and good memories, until other revelations were imparted to him, dark things, things he would be asked to do with this new mantle. Images traced through his consciousness with such speed and force that he began to fear for his own sanity.

He shuddered, considering what this could all mean before it was through.

But before that thought could consume him, the simple ritual was at an end, and he felt peace in his heart like the calm of still waters.

When Dossolum finished speaking, he gently urged Palamon to his feet, a fatherly smile on his face. "I know the peace that rests in your heart at this moment, my friend. May it ever be so. You must, however, remember this, that as a man your rendering of the Will can only come at the expenditure of your own spirit."

"I know this, Dossolum. What are you telling me?" Palamon asked.

Dossolum smiled. "Balance, my friend. It is about balance. When you choose to draw upon the Will, it requires a measure of your own Forda to give that rendering life. So be judicious in your use of this gift, as the greater your rendering act, the greater the price to your own spirit, your energy . . . your Forda. It will take a physical toll, and as intercessor, there will be multitudes who will call upon you for help. You will have, sometimes, to say no."

Palamon nodded, a vague unease now in his heart. They resumed looking out over the expanse that fell away from their high place. And just before the Greater Light fled the sky entirely, Dossolum said with a tired fondness, "Your work as a servant now has new meaning, my friend. What you have done for me, now do for them."

The words were lost to the whir of crickets. The chill on Palamon's skin, he thought, came not only from the cold of night.

CR8O

NEWS OF THE FOUNDERS' decision to abandon their labors had spread like fire. A week ago, Palamon had stood with Dossolum and been given the power to render the Will and made intercessor. Now, he rushed down the marble colonnades of the tabernacle. The great pillars rose majestically on either side of him, ending at the open sky. In the marble surfaces everywhere were recorded the many feats and designs and efforts of the council to bring forth worlds and give place to men to learn and grow. Many of these Palamon himself had chiseled with painstaking care.

Today he hurried past it all, hastening to the central chamber, having called the council to convene to hear his plea.

Fear and uncertainty had swept Estem Salo. Palamon, chief among the Sheason, had requested a formal audience with the Framers and Dossolum, who he saw first as he entered the council chamber.

"Palamon," said the Voice of the Council, "we will hear you because of your long and faithful service, but there are pressing matters to attend to. We do not have much time."

Palamon did not hesitate. "Stop this. Don't allow the taint of one council member's efforts to cause your ill-faith in an entire world. It needn't be so. Please."

Dossolum stood. "The vote to abandon this labor has been made, Palamon. It was not a debate. The entire council, save Maldea, is in agreement. We did not rush to judgment in this, my friend. We have long contended with Maldea over his efforts here. We've tried to turn back what he has done. And we do know what it will mean to this world that we must leave our work here unfinished. But we find this to be the best course."

"Why?" Palamon asked. "I don't understand."

The Voice of the Council stood looking at him, seeming to consider how much he should say. Finally, he gave a slight nod of acquiescence. "You know, my friend, the first eternal truth: that Forza and Forda, matter and energy, can be neither created nor destroyed, only rendered, changed. The council could remain on this world, spend years, perhaps an age, trying to undo the imbalance

Maldea has wrought." Dossolum paused, looking more distraught, more *human* than Palamon ever remembered seeing him. In a softer voice, he continued, "But it would be irresponsible of us. It would not be a good use of the Will."

"To save the lives of so many—"

"Palamon," Dossolum interrupted, "We lament the choice. We care about those to whom we give the breath of life. But the council must weigh the cost of its use of Forda I'Forza. It must decide whether, on balance, it is better to expend so much effort in repairing what is so far damaged, or whether more may be accomplished by expending that same effort to build something new or care for a world that has not such overpowering corruption."

"But you are many, and Maldea is but one," Palamon countered.

Dossolum said only, "Maldea's gifts are great, my friend." His words echoed in the Tabernacle of the Sky like a malediction.

"Have you ever deserted the children you've given life to, ever once in all your immortal lives? Think on that. If you permit yourselves now to be dissuaded from treading the rough course ahead, how much easier will it be to do the next time? Your offices are sacred and perilous. I implore you, stand fast in your duty now. There are so many of your children, that I cannot count the lives that depend upon it."

In a soft voice of warning, Dossolum said, "Take care, Palamon."

But he could not. Manoa was gone, the intercessor who spoke to the Council of Creation for the people. He had been slaughtered by the very thing to which these Founders now had chosen to abandon their young world.

"I will not!" he declared. "I will be damned before I remain silent. The mighty work of your own hands toils in the fields you've given them; they look up at the Sky when they seek peace, and eagerly await the knowledge you impart to provide the path for their growth. It is unthinkable that you would shut them away from your grace and leave them to a world now fraught with unimaginable peril. How can you be so heartless?"

"Be STILL!" Dossolum commanded.

Palamon froze. The echoes of the council Voice rippled every surface of the tabernacle.

When the quaking abated, Palamon made a fateful decision. He would risk all, since to live afterward if he did not would be a hell of his own making. With quiet intent he drew the Will for the very first time, pushing a barrier of calm out from his body, the quietude expanding slowly, gently, until it filled the Tabernacle of the Sky.

It was not a rendering to inflict or compel, but simply to impart the honesty and hope of what he would next ask. Many on the council nodded in silent appreciation of the restoration of serenity which typically abided in the tabernacle.

With a final thought of what he risked, Palamon addressed the men and women seated at the great semi-circular table. "If you will not keep this world in your embrace, and finish what you have begun, then at least give them some means whereby they may rescue themselves."

Given gently, earnestly, Palamon's words, he knew, were also an indictment. But not one, he could see, that the council would deny. Though they remained steadfast in their course, his plea touched the air in the same way Dossolum's words had so recently done . . . but with an undeniable compassion.

The members of the council looked around at one another, seeming to come to agreement without the need of words. Dossolum nodded, and soon his face showed the familiar smile.

"You remind us of our purpose, Palamon. Thank you." He looked up at the great open sky above the council chamber and drew a long breath. "We will yet abandon this labor. It is a hard choice, but the right one. What has transpired here is irreparable without inordinate use of the Will and the rendering of matter and energy. You may trust that shortly we will deal with Maldea for his crimes. But for your sake, we will see the vile breeds given life by his hand placed in the outlands far from the family of man. There we will seal them with their creator, never to return. We will make mortals accountable for the maintenance of the veil that holds these creations at bay. And still other instruments of power, even the Charter itself, we will put in place here because you have hope for them, where we do not."

A feeling of agreement, contentment, filled the air. The council, Palamon could tell, was pleased with itself.

But there was still more he must say.

"A man may eat, and be warm, and remain relatively safe from the menace of the world he treads, but if he has no hope . . . he is dead." Palamon looked directly at Dossolum, realizing he spoke as much for himself as for the people he now served as intercessor. "The faith we have offered them will be hollow when you leave, Dossolum. They will learn of this abandonment, and their hearts will grow hard—a hardness they will turn against one another, despite the exile of Maldea's fiends beyond some veil. What will they believe in?"

Dossolum looked back, his eyes intent but kind. "Does there need to be a god for belief to be valid and meaningful and . . . powerful, Palamon? Perhaps, my friend, that is precisely what belief *is* . . . having faith even when you are uncertain."

The simple truth of it struck him, and yet the reasoning broke down in one tragic respect. "But who will answer them, when they lift their voices in prayer?"

The Voice of the Council looked at Palamon with a knowing expression, but said nothing. It was then that Palamon knew the reason for his ill-feeling at the moment he'd been given the authority to render the Will and made intercessor. He bowed deeply in gratitude and deference, and left the Tabernacle of the Sky, realizing his choices had lasting consequences for one other.

c૩εっ

THROUGHOUT THE EVENING after his audience with the council, Palamon said nothing, holding back any questions or deep discussion with Solera. He wanted one last normal night with his companion. He meant only to see to the uncomplicated straightening of their small home, conversation over less important things, and one last night of love-making before he told her, before things changed for her, for them.

Throughout the course of the evening he often found himself gazing at her, acutely aware of her fair skin, deep auburn hair, and penetrating brown eyes. After so long, he still felt physically drawn to her. And as much for her keen mind as her beauty.

Solera, like him, had ascended to the office of Sheason. She served Anais, the second voice of the council. But his affection for her had nothing to do with the strength of her service, or even her

101

beauty, but rather his fondness for her came first for her good humor. Perhaps, he thought, because he was, as Dossolum reminded him, a serious man.

But they'd found joy in each other's company and in the sharing of their Sheason calling, and had known love for many years, supporting the labors of the Great Ones in fashioning this world.

And yet, the grand designs toward which they worked each day seemed less important when they spent time together discussing the rain or wind or the power in language, not to create—as the Founders made use of it—but to thrill and inspire. Theirs was a love affair that had sustained Palamon for longer than he could remember. But tonight he feared the question they must discuss, one they could no longer avoid.

In the afterglow of long and tender love-making, they lay together in a grove of blooming aspen—their place—beneath the Lesser Light, the perspiration cool on their skin as they stared up.

"What is on your mind, Palamon?" Solera asked. "You've held it through all our quiet talk and love. Now unburden yourself."

In the dark, he smiled. Somehow he'd known she would see through him. Still, he'd wanted this before . . .

"You've heard of the Framers' abandonment," he said, believing she surely must be aware.

"And I heard that you went and pleaded for those being left behind. You can take heart that you did what you could."

"I am no martyr," he said. "The Founders still intend to abandon their labors here."

"We are wise, you and I, and have toiled much to aid this work, but we are not gods, Palamon. You must trust their wisdom." She drew his face around to look directly at him. "Have you considered that they entrusted you with the same authority they possess to call on the Will? It is the first power, Palamon. The other powers of language and song and movement and all the rest are connected to the Will, each in their own way. But the power to render the Will is its purest, most direct use. What Dossolum has done for you is give that power more purpose, as you serve as intercessor."

Palamon sat up, dreading what he must tell her. "Solera, I don't believe Dossolum conferred this office on me to simply serve as intercessor."

She sat up beside him. The wind soughed lightly through the trees, caressing their shoulders. "Why else, Palamon?"

He looked at her, feeling the bitterness of knowing his next words would change everything. He had hoped it wouldn't come to this. "I've studied the ways of the Will, Solera. And though I've not yet rendered much, I'd thought I would always use it to uphold the principles that give life its meaning . . ."

Solera's brow furrowed. "Palamon?"

He did not want to say it. Even now part of him resisted. But he had procrastinated long enough. "Solera, it is clear to me now. Dossolum granted me this authority not simply to aid others, maybe not even *first* to aid others . . .

"Then why?" she asked

He gave her a long, pained look. "To carry it into battle."

He watched as understanding bloomed in her face, perhaps a hint of anger, but finally a sadness that left her countenance looking tired. She put her head on his shoulder and wept. Silent tears fell and ran down his chest.

Palamon's heart broke. It broke because of the change that would follow for all the Sheason and all the creation given life by the hands of the Founders; but more than any of this, his heart broke because here forward, Solera would live her life in fear that Palamon could be killed by virtue of the very gift that set him apart.

She drew back, her beauty bathed in the moonlight, tears shining on her cheeks. "We will be all right," she said.

He wanted to tell her not to worry. But it would be a lie. When the council completed the placing of all Maldea's hellish creations and raised the veil, they would move on, and he would be left here in their place.

Unable to speak, he nodded. And they held each other in their grove of aspen all night. Only when the birds of morn sang out their melodies did they rise and return to their home. A small part of him ached for her to ask him not to carry the mantle Dossolum had given him for this benighted world.

How can this be right?

He could only hope that the difference he could make here would justify whatever sacrifices he and his love would be called upon to make.

Sensing his mortality already coming upon him, he felt the bitter irony of the words he had uttered to Solera only hours ago: *I am no martyr.*

He might live . . . and die . . . to prove those words false.

Once in their home again, he caught her in another embrace and said finally, "We will be all right."

She pushed him back gently. "I'll hold you to it," she said, and smiled. Then, to begin this new—this last—chapter of their lives, she took the vase and went to refresh it with more long-stemmed, fresh-cut grass. The light, clean smell of it, their simple, delicate forms, Palamon decided, were just the right tokens of the years ahead.

෦ඊ෨

PALAMON SAT AT THE table near the front window of their home, writing. A forlorn feeling had settled over him. It had been days since the council had departed the world. The door to their house stood open, as it had done all the while. He had listened while the other Sheason said their farewells in the streets beyond that door. He'd been unable to go out and say goodbye—not for bitterness' sake, but because there'd been nothing left to say.

It hadn't been long after that that most of the Sheason departed Estem Salo for new lives in distant parts of this world they'd helped to form.

Now, an eerie silence had settled over Estem Salo. Once, he could have sat on his front porch and fairly heard the sound of quills moving over dry parchment in the archives a hundred strides down the road. It wasn't really so, but the palpable feeling of thought and preparation and scholarship made Palamon *think* he heard their instruments even now recording it all and framing the development of these lands, these people. They were pleasant thoughts.

At the moment, his mind was as quiet as was the small town where now he and Solera were among the few Sheason left, trying to know what next to do. He hadn't bothered to return to the tabernacle. He'd go eventually; perhaps there was wisdom to glean from what the Founders had left behind. But not yet; he couldn't go there yet.

The Voice of the Council had promised to put in place the means for mankind to protect and (perhaps also, Palamon hoped) redeem itself. These things had been written in a single, thin volume discreetly placed on a windowsill during the few hours he had managed to sleep in those first days after the council's decision to abandon this world. It sat there still.

He hadn't opened the book, which came wrapped in a black, brushed leather case, lashed with another length of hide. The note tucked into the lash has been penned in Dossolum's neat script; Palamon knew what it was. His heart gladdened slightly to have it. But he would only find any real joy in it much later, though even then, he knew, the hope the Founders offered would be improbable and difficult. *Perhaps impossible.* But for now, utter silence and aloneness had descended on them like a condemnation.

Mostly, he preferred it this way. He needed to mourn; before he'd be any good to the people he'd stayed behind to help, he needed to purge the bitterness he felt toward the council. He had spoken with only one man since *the Abandonment*, as they were calling it: Efram, the man whom Palamon had tried to help some time ago. Efram had told him of a spreading hopelessness in the people. The abandonment had gotten inside everyone . . .

As he sat, wondering what he would do next, the sound of boots on the pebbled road rose in the stillness. He stood, knowing whom he would see when he walked out his door.

From the far end of the main road through Estem Salo, the tall form of Jo'ha'nel approached. He moved with a strange grace, as though he'd somehow escaped the mortality that fell to those left here when the Founders departed. This other Sheason came at him with an intent he could see and feel, and Palamon found himself instinctively readying the Will.

Then the dark Sheason stopped. "They've left you behind," he said, smiling unkindly.

"I've *chosen* to stay behind," Palamon corrected. "The Founders had their reasons for leaving, but I would not abandon this world's people to their own ignorance. You could help me," Palamon added. "You are knowledgeable, and you bear the power to draw on the Will; we could help them find their way."

The other laughed. "Would you help me rescue those also left behind inside your Founders' Bourne? We could undo this veil, find unity and peace among those beings created by both Maldea and Dossolum."

Palamon knew it was not a genuine offer. "I have seen the appetite of those given life by Maldea. There can be no peace between them and those who live south and east. You know this." He stopped, peering into the hard face of his former brother. "Why have you chosen this path, Jo'ha'nel? Especially now that Maldea has been sealed away. You have nothing to fear from him. Come. Let us build something here."

A silence fell across Estem Salo for several long moments. Then the dark Sheason spoke again, "I told you that you must decide on which side to stand. It is time. Who will you now serve? Those who've left you with broken promises, and gone on to start again somewhere else? Or the Founder they have left behind on *this* world?"

Palamon's thoughts turned first to the image of a young girl crying and holding her dead baby brother in her lap. Then he saw Efram's wife, lying dead despite his attempts to save her. And finally, in his mind he could see Manoa's lifeless body on the steps of the tabernacle. He recalled thinking over and over . . . *not yet. Not yet for violence, and hate.* But looking up the road of Estem Salo, Palamon knew the time had finally come for these things.

He shook his head. "I serve none of these," he said. "I will serve mankind."

Bitterness filled Jo'ha'nel's countenance. Before Palamon could say or do anything more, an unseen force traversed the space between him and the dark Sheason, ripping him off the ground and sending him back hard against the side of his house. He fell to the ground, and felt the warmth of blood coming fast from a gash in his scalp. Without thinking or standing, he slammed his fists together in a rage and focused his anger at his new enemy. The earth itself erupted in a violent geyser of rocks and soil that sent Jo'ha'nel shooting ten paces skyward.

The other landed heavily, but staggered to his feet with a manic look in his eye and a mad grin on his lips. Then he stopped, stood still, and closed his eyes. The earth, suddenly bitingly cold, creaked all around Palamon. His flesh began to blister and freeze, his blood feeling cold in his veins. He fell onto his side, the shallow breaths he exhaled pluming as though he lay in a winter storm. He could feel his heart slowing and ice forming over his eyes.

Palamon had a fleeting thought. *I could let go.* If he did, the pain of the abandonment by the ancients who'd covenanted to this world . . . would simply disappear, as his Forda left his body, relieving him of consciousness.

He would welcome the end of this emptiness but for one thing. Palamon—and Solera— had already made the sacrifices that had caused in him this abject spirit. After it all, he would not throw away those sacrifices by conceding to a Sheason who had forsaken his calling.

Holding onto this indignation, Palamon raised a plam toward Jo'ha'nel and spoke a few words of the conceivers' tongue. Flame erupted around the fiendish renderer, licking hungrily at his flesh and raiment. From where he lay, Palamon, too, felt the heat, and thawed enough to sit up against the side of his home. The thought that he had taken life spread like poison in his mind, and he shook his head in denial.

Then, as Palamon watched the conflagration, Jo'ha'nel walked unscathed from the fire, his emaciated body and wide shoulders bearing toward Palamon in a graceful nightmarish gait. The dark Sheason then brayed a few words of his own, the sound fouling the air and driving the breath from Palamon's lungs. All his senses leapt, sending stabbing pain into his mind, and all leading to a white roaring rush.

Palamon again thought this might be the end. And he, the only barrier between this vile Sheason and the already hopeless people still hanging onto life across the great wide of this world.

While he struggled against the onslaught, simultaneously fighting off despair, Solera rushed into the street between him and Jo'ha'nel and raised a defiant cry.

"Stop this! You have no reason to bring death here. Neither Palamon nor the people you torment and rape and murder have earned your scorn." She pointed toward the heavens. "If you must be angry, it should be with those who no longer walk this earth. But I will not stand idle while you torture—"

Solera's words were instantly cut short. Her body rose off the ground as she clutched at her throat. She rotated so that she lay parallel to the road, suspended three strides high in the air . . . and began to spin.

It all happened so fast. And even as Palamon struggled to stand, the fire he had called to burn Jo'ha'nel streamed like a sinuous river toward Solera and engulfed her body. She became a whirling maelstrom of flame and hot wind and strangled cries. And in just seconds, the blaze flared and went out, dropping a spray of dark heavy ash.

"NO!" The sound tore through Estem Salo.

Palamon raged. Forgotten were the dull burning thoughts inside the white rushing sound that had filled his mind: worries over the Abandonment, or even Jo'ha'nel's abandonment of the promise of his service to the people he now preyed upon.

He would later grieve for those things. But not now. Now, his heart knew only wrath! And with it, the noise and rushing ceased, the hate that exuded from the dark Sheason was pushed back upon him, and Palamon stood.

He did not waver, but began to stride toward Jo'ha'nel, indignation giving him new strength. A flicker of concern passed over the other's face as Palamon raised his hands. He thrust them violently toward Jo'ha'nel and sent him flying twenty strides, where he fell roughly onto the road.

The trees bristled; window glass shattered; birds squawked and fluttered, disturbed in flight. The retaliation continued to emanate from Palamon in waves, descending on Jo'ha'nel in brutalizing blows meant to crush but not kill, to cause an intensity of suffering that would make him plead for the mercy of a fast death.

Sharp cries of agony rose into the still blue skies

But as Palamon tried to prolong the attack, his own Forda waned, and like the dark that follows an extinguished candle, his assault abruptly ended and he fell to the road, entirely spent.

He watched as Jo'ha'nel, lying upon the ground, gave him a spiteful look and managed to spread his fingers out over the dirt. As Palamon looked, the soil there parched, whitened, then burned, sizzling as a thin crust of glass spread over a wide circle around his former brother.

Palamon realized in horror what Jo'ha'nel had done; he'd drawn the Forda from the very earth, stealing it for his own—one of the basest violations of the Charter, putting matter and spirit out of balance. But with the heinous act, he had renewed himself. Invigorated, he promptly stood, and began to advance on Palamon.

But Palamon had nothing more to give, his spirit so drained that he could only watch the slow approach of his enemy, and prepare for death.

I gave my all. I go to the next life content . . . and to meet you there, my love . . .

He closed his eyes, ready for either a crushing blow or some other use of the Will that would end his life, when a hoarse scream shot up the road from beyond the archive. Palamon opened his eyes and managed to turn his head in the direction of the sound. At a dead run came the one man he had met in the lowlands that he had so often spied from his promontory with Dossolum. Efram, who held in one hand a long club and in the other a forked farming implement, and who barreled toward them with fear in his eyes but no shortage of courage.

Jo'ha'nel shifted his ireful gaze up toward the intruder, a wicked gleam in his eye as he seemed to relish the chance to murder another of these pitiful men. But before Jo'ha'nel could render the Will, Efram hurled his pitchfork at the dark Sheason, as though he'd practiced doing so.

The farm tool sailed through the blue sky, spinning slightly, Efram's aim seeming true. Jo'ha'nel, so caught off guard, watched as fascinated as Palamon, until it was too late, and the sharp spines pierced his upper leg, driving the iron tines deep into his flesh.

Maldea's first Sheason looked down at the wound and howled, the force of it sending a rush of wind from his mouth. It blasted Palamon's cheeks and neck. But before Jo'ha'nel could look up to send Efram to his earth, the farmer beset him, pummeling the malefactor with his wooden club. The dark Sheason fell and writhed, trying to roll away. Efram kept on him until Palamon spoke.

Too weak to call out, he coughed the words, "No . . . stop."

Efram's arm paused high in mid-blow, and he slowly lowered his cudgel as though suddenly returning to his senses. He heaved deep breaths and came to a knee beside Palamon.

"You look bad. Are you in pain?" the farmer asked.

"I'll be all right." He looked at his home, and felt—even then—that it was not a place to which he ever wanted to return. But it did hold something he needed. "In my house, on the windowsill there is a ledger. Bring it to me."

Efram moved quickly, and returned a few moments later with the gift from Dossolum. He handed the ledger to Palamon, who took it and held it tight against his chest. Whatever words it contained would be the last he would have from his friend on the council—a mixed blessing.

"What about him?" Efram thrust his cudgel toward Jo'ha'nel.

"I will kill him myself," Palamon said, his voice like the dry husks of Efram's fields.

But when he looked up, the dark Sheason was gone. Efram stood staring down the road, a bit slack-jawed. Jo'ha'nel would return, but not today.

Palamon then looked at the road a few strides away, dusted with black ash . . . the remains of Solera. The reality of her death descended on him in a crushing wave, and he cried out.

He did not know how long he lay there, lost in his grief, before he found the presence of mind to say, "Take me to the Archive," and point south. He knew he would mourn more later, but he could feel his own life ebbing, and all that had happened, including Solera's death, would come to naught if he didn't take some immediate action.

As Efram picked up Palamon and carried him to the archive, the servant of Dossolum felt a dark revelation take root in his heart: Jo'ha'nel had abandoned one of the first tenets of the Charter of this world, something written upon the walls of the archive almost from the beginning: the power to render the Will had to be drawn from the spirit of the one calling its use. But it wasn't as much the fact that Jo'ha'nel had violated this sacred trust—though that would have earned him the severest of punishments had he done so when Dossolum yet tarried here—but the fact that the Founders had spoken this principle so early on, having it recorded . . . as though they anticipated a world where its inhabitants would have need to *make use* of the Will.

Why?

Palamon found his thoughts tied up in secrets he couldn't untangle. And though he finally left them alone, an uneasy feeling remained deep in his heart, as he wondered what Dossolum might have known from the very beginning.

Inside the archive, the stillness did not help Palamon's mood—this had been a place of thought and great industry. Indeed, if there were answers to questions like those he'd just let go, they would have been pursued and ultimately discovered here.

Efram gently sat Palamon down at a table.

"In the cabinet," he said with a strained voice. "The cedar box."

The farmer went straightaway, returning with the Sheason's personal case. Palamon opened it with trembling fingers and drew out a sprig drawn from a special grove quite distant from the Tabernacle of the Sky or Estem Salo. He placed it on his tongue and allowed it to dissolve. In just moments new energy spread through him, bringing fresh pain as his body awakened to its own damage; he welcomed it as a reminder that he had survived.

Then Palamon drew out a small journal. Before setting it all down—everything from the moment he'd found Manoa splayed across the tabernacle steps, to his return to a vacant archive—he turned to Efram.

"Thank you," he said. "You have my undying gratitude."

The farmer replied, "What must we do?"

Palamon thought. How to begin the last stages of forming this world without the help of the First Fathers? When a spontaneous smile touched his cheeks it felt good. Perhaps he would find his humor and delight after all, in simply a different way.

"My friend, bring others here. I will begin to teach them: to read, to write, to remember. Some, even, will take up the ways of the Sheason." He nodded, mostly to himself. "And with time, and industry, and holding to what we know is right and true—" *and those things left to me in Dossolum's ledger*—"we will continue on." He looked up at Efram. "And we will find some small bit of glory along the way if we try, Efram." *If we try.*

CIVIL WAR
FROM TRIAL OF INTENTIONS
BOOK TWO
OF
THE VAULT OF HEAVEN

INTRODUCTION

WHEN I FINISHED WITH the first draft of *Trial of Intentions*, it was massive—500,000 words.

I began to cut.

Actually, there were a couple of rounds of cutting. In the final round, the following scene was one of the last to go. I like the scene. It's a good showing for the characters, and it dials up the tension.

And yet . . . I didn't really need it.

There's a scene that comes not long after it that accomplishes much the same thing, but also does more heavy lifting in terms of setting up conflict in future volumes of the series. Plus, a new magic is introduced. So, I pulled this chapter.

I've had a lot of notes from readers who knew I'd been on a journey from that 500,000 words. They've been interested to know what was being edited out. So, I thought I'd share. And what you have here is pre-edit, before I submitted the manuscript to my editor. So, you're getting a look at the underbelly of the manuscript, too.

Stuff I dig here? The general's battle command office is très cool, for my money. I mean, his map has figures that move and disappear based on battle movements. I need one of those.

I also dig Roth. He's a consummate politician. I love writing him, even if he's a bastard. A well-intentioned bastard, sure. But still . . .

CIVIL WAR

FAR BEHIND HIM, dark smoke still curled into the sky from the burning Bastulan Cathedral, while Roth moved into Recityv's garrison district. This quarter of the city stood in perfect cleanliness and order. No idlers, no indolence. As he made his way across a broad compound, he noted that men here strode with a snap in their step, real purpose. A few of these spared him a glance, suspicion and dislike clear on their faces—either at the sight of him or the League emblem on his chestnut brown cloak. He smiled in return—respect took many forms.

The garrison stone—granite quarried south out of the Lesule mountains—was several shades lighter than the rock used in the palace and other courts of Solath Mahnus. But that made sense. A standing army of this size in Recityv was a relatively new thing, going back maybe thirty generations. Before that, a fighting force of this magnitude had been raised only when there'd been need. But Roth liked the look of the stone. The quarters and supply houses and assembly halls of the garrison district seemed sharp and ready and new—something Roth could appreciate.

Down a broad causeway, stable yards and drill fields were occupied by cavalry and footmen honing their war trade. Roth turned the opposite direction, where the street ended at a modest building he knew served as headquarters for the army and home of its commander, General Van Steward.

The posted sentry eyed Roth as he approached. Before the guard could speak, Roth waved a hand. "The general is expecting me, and I am already late."

He mounted the few steps to the front door, but the man stepped into his path anyway. "No, sir. I will call on the general. Wait here, please."

Roth frowned, but nodded. He turned and stood looking down the long concourse toward the practice fields and the maneuvers being run today. He loved the efficiency of training, the rule of order and martial mandate that permeated the garrison. He would never admit it to Van Steward, but he'd modeled much of the League's own discipline after the general's strict regimentation.

A moment later, the door behind him opened again, and Van Steward stepped out, taking a stance beside him. While Roth continued to watch the army drill, the general's gaze rose up over the quarters to the left where billows of black smoke lazed distantly into the sky.

"Why do I believe you had something to do with that?" Van Steward said coolly.

"Because you trust only those you command," Roth said without pause. "And your dislike for me is hardly a secret."

"Your half right," the general replied. "Braceman Paleer." Presently the sentry returned. "Take three squads and find the origin of that smoke." Van Steward pointed. "If the fire brigade needs assistance, you will assist. And get word to the Regent and her Emerit

Guard. They need to mind her safety until we know what this is. Go."

The braceman left immediately at a dead run. *Such efficiency and obedience.* The solider disappeared around the corner. "We have things to discuss," Roth said.

"Yes, we do," the general returned curtly.

Roth tried not to show his surprise or interest. He disliked Van Steward for his cur-like allegiance to the old woman, Regent Helaina Storalaith. Strictly speaking, it *was* perhaps appropriate for the Recityv general to kowtow to the city's regent. But with Helaina it was something more. Maybe a fondness that trespassed the lines of propriety. No matter. All Roth needed to know was whether the General stood by the law of his command or the friendships that accompanied his post. Soon—if Roth was successful—remaining loyal to both would be a difficult thing to manage.

Before they left the portico, Van Steward pointed again in the direction of the smoke. "Whoever set that is bold. And foolish."

"Why is that?" Roth asked.

"I wouldn't want to have the Dannire looking for me," the general said, a wicked thin grin on his face.

He was truly surprised. "What? The old story about holy warriors? A few heedless sword-bearers, fighting in the name of dead gods? Those Dannire?" He smiled.

"If I was the arsonist of Bastulan, I would fear even the idea of the Dannire. Let alone the stories that make children believe the gods sanction murder." Van Steward nodded toward the smoke. "I'm not sure the arsonist who got that blaze going was thinking too far ahead."

Roth left it there. Though, talk of the Dannire did give him an idea he'd put aside for later consideration. He followed Van Steward inside and through a wide receiving hall into the military command office. The walls rose ten strides high, each one no less than twenty strides long. The walls themselves had been hand-painted with maps of the Eastlands. Nations and kingdoms were rendered in geographic detail, with numbers and brief notes scrawled here and there: populations, export goods, trade routes, governing bodies, names and ranks of in-country leaders.

In the center of the room stood a great table, ten paces on a side. Its surface had likewise been meticulously painted to reflect a map of the Eastlands. Across the broad atlas, small figurines stood, clearly reflecting military positions. In Kamas, Masson Dimn, and Ebon, groups of the little statues seemed to indicate sizeable armies. The Wynstout Dominion had its share, too, but they were widely dispersed.

While Roth looked on, Van Steward picked up off the table a long, straight rod with a short T at the end. He consulted an open letter resting near the edge of the great chart, and then used the rod to push two of the figurines from the plain north of Sever Ens toward the hills that bordered Alon'Itol. His face darkened as he considered the move.

Seemingly forgotten, Roth idled near the wall map of Elyk Divad, and noticed several protruding nails tied with red ribbons. Many of the wall maps had the same. He fingered one of the ribbons. "And what are these?"

Without looking up, the general answered, "Quiet sightings." He said it with a hint of challenge.

"Really. And you lend these *sightings* credibility?" Roth tugged at another ribbon.

"Some are from my own patrols. My men don't lie." Van Steward crossed to an adjacent wall and raised the rod he held to point up at another map, near the Saecula Forest. "The Pall has been crossed more and more often in recent months. The Convocation is necessary."

"Are you implying that I don't agree?" Roth moved to a leather bound chair set before the general's table-desk and sat.

"You have openly refused to acknowledge the threat of the Bourne. The resurgence of the Quiet is why the Regent recalls Convocation. And you hate Helaina. So, no, I'm not *implying*."

As Van Steward passed the large table map that dominated the center of the room, two of the figures situated in the Soliel Stretches disappeared from sight. They'd both seen it. And they shared a knowing look at the fading of the simulacra from the war map. The atlas's strange quality had showed them that a legion, probably Far, had just perished. Most of the statuettes still standing in the Soliel could only represent Quiet.

The general moved to the other side of his desk, but did not sit. The man's deeply scarred face reminded Roth that threats would not prevail here. He must keep his composure, stay fixed on the outcome. He started with a different kind of smile—a guard-down lets-be-honest kind.

"I support the recalling of the Convocation, general. I just don't agree with the Regent's motivation. But I've not come to debate the merits of red ribbons."

"Then before you state your purpose, I will state mine." The general came around the desk and leaned back against it directly in front of Roth, taking a close position, hovering over him. *Nicely done, general. The power of proximity and relative position over your opponent.*

"Please do," Roth said, crossing his legs and speaking in an easy, conversational manner. He loved the politic game.

Van Steward's brow creased in distaste. *Good.* "Ascendant Staned," Van Steward began, striking a formal tone, "your society is overstepping its authority in matters of law and personal conduct. While well-intentioned, your Leaguemen behave as sanctioned gendarmes, which they are not."

"We have the right—"

"To uphold the law." Van Steward completed Roth's rote response to this criticism. "Yes, I know. But they walk the streets with the League crest emblazoned on their cloaks, casting critical eyes on the citizens, and enforcing their own interpretation of the law. It has created confusion, and undermines the Regent's authority."

"You mean *your* authority," Roth said, tilting his head in subtle condescension.

The general stared at him for several moments, composed but obviously tiring of their conversation. "The people see two *separate* authorities they must answer to."

Roth maintained his good-mannered smile. "And those are . . ."

Van Steward did not take the bait. "I will assume it's only the league's zeal that has caused it to misrepresent itself to the people. But after this discussion, you will correct this zeal, Am I understood?"

Roth's good humor slipped away. He fought his instinct to stand and defy Van Steward, challenge him to try and thwart the civility the League sought to give men. Instead, he only stared up into the general's ruined face, and let his anger cool.

At last, his composure returned, he could speak smartly. "May I come to my purpose in visiting you on this morning when Recityv burns?"

"After you answer my question: Am I understood?"

"You are . . . *understood*," Roth echoed. *If not obeyed.*

"I am listening, then." Van Steward folded his arms, as if preparing to refute whatever Roth meant to say. The general really was quite predictable. But then, such was his charm.

"Thank you." Roth now stood, removing Van Steward's advantage of superior position. He paced around the chair he'd been sitting in, and dramatically drew it aside, removing any barrier between them, as a challenger is wont to do. Then he adopted a gracious smile—better politics.

"The Regent was once a strong leader. It may even have been her decision to annex west Wynstout that made me want to be a leader myself. Terribly gutsy move, that. But I've also made no secret of my issues with the Regent's policies and decisions of late." He allowed a touch of sadness in his eyes and tone. "She grows fatuous and impractical, General. Surely, you see this, too. Or does your friendship with her cloud the objectivity needed from *your* office?"

"A question requiring a careful answer: Damn myself or damn the Regent." Van Steward offered a bitter smile. "I will say this, Staned, you are a better politician than Helaina."

"Thank—"

"It was not a compliment," Van Steward quickly followed. "The answer to your question is that I serve the interests of the city, of Vohnce. And officially, I believe the Regent is sharper now that I've ever seen her. She has to be. There are vipers all around. She must be safe or be bitten."

"You've a sharp tongue yourself, General," Roth complimented genuinely. "But you can't have it both ways. The Regent is old. I hate to say it, but we've passed the point where her age can be excused as valuable experience. These last few seasons, her judgment has lapsed. It's the same for all of our elder statesmen. Age gets the best of us. We lose the ability to discern—" Roth stopped abruptly at the sight of the general's incredulous smile. The laugh lines in the man's face tugged at the scars there.

"It's interesting that only you seem to find this fault with Helaina. The other members of the council sing her praises for finding solutions to—"

"Don't grow too comfortable in the rule of the majority. The winds of allegiance do change suddenly in a storm." Roth held his own smile.

The general stood up from his desk-table. "I will note and distribute to the Council my fair warning to you of the League's impropriety in administering justice. Once that is done, my men will be instructed to arrest any Leagueman seen taking action toward a citizen beyond the humanitarian and advocacy tenets of your own creed."

Roth closed the gap between himself and Van Steward. The time for diplomacy and politics was past. Authority must be claimed.

"If your Quietgiven threat is real, it will require steel to stand against it. If it is only rumor and legend and folktales, we will need reform and new ideas to replace antiquated fears." He drew closer still to Van Steward, so that he could smell the morning's gravy on his breath, and see clearly the scar tissue in his cheek. "These are not the qualities of your Regent. Her genteel benevolence has served its purpose, but its time is past. Lines will be drawn. Council members will be forced to choose a path."

"And will you be drawing those lines, Leagueman? Will you be forcing the choice?" Van Steward's anger was palpable. This was no garrison general; this was a man who had risen to command through blood and battle. He stared back with the threat of real violence.

Roth could still smell the smoke of Bastulan in his cloak. A portrait of flames lingered in his mind.

His voice came low and sure when he spoke. "I will."

The two glared at one another, surrounded in the war hall by the maps of nations and red ribbons hailing the encroachment of Quiet that Roth knew more about than he would ever admit.

But he had work to do. Work begun long ago. He'd taken another step that morning by making a pyre of Bastulan. And here, now, in the war room of Recityv, he tested an allegiance that he would need if he meant to continue that work.

Resuming his casual smile, he added, "Take care not to fall down on the wrong side of those lines, General."

Before Roth could stop it, Van Steward thrust him to the floor and stood with a boot on his throat, slowly pressing down. "You should know that intimidation has no place in my war room. And threatening an officer of the army is a punishable offense. Is that what you were doing, Leagueman?"

Roth glared up at him, and struggled to speak. "I came to discuss a matter of state. I will bring a vote to the council on Helaina's ability to continue as Regent. Those loyal to her will be forced to resign their seats on the Council."

Van Steward pressed down once, hard, then relaxed his boot. "My men will not follow you, Roth. And neither will I. Our honor won't permit it."

Your idealism is commendable, but obsolete. "I think you are in danger of having your own men remove you to the prisons of Solath Mahnus . . . striking a member of the High Council."

"I think testimony would show you fell under my boot." The general pressed down once more, for emphasis, then removed his foot from Roth's throat.

He got to his feet, rubbing his neck. "These are perilous times, General. But not for the reasons you track on your walls and map table." He gestured broadly at the room. "Generations have grown up to inherit little more from their parents than superstition, fear of the unknown. Their traditions are based on myths that are no longer relevant, and values of leadership that turn on patronage more than progress. Great resources go to sustain your army, and when was the last real need we had of it. My men with their emblem on their cloaks do a better job of ensuring the public safety than your gendarmes. And for all the rumors, what threat has marched on Recityv? There are people starving in our alleyways, low professions in profusion, and drug-addled minds committing petty crimes too numerous to record. Where is your army in all of this, general?" Roth smiled as he said it.

Van Steward looked back, unfazed. "No martial presence can make goodness compulsory, Leagueman. If that is your aim, you've failed before you begin."

Roth laughed harshly. "General, you are too much a part of the world that is moving on to see the change. There is unrest all around us. And no answer is forthcoming from Helaina, or even her vaunted Estem Salo. Instead our Regent holds private meetings with superstitious old men. Do you see the danger?" he asked with subtle condescension. "Dead gods, man, stand up. If your reports are accurate, will you follow a diplomat . . . an aging woman to war? You make me afraid, Bolermy."

"Of that, I am not sorry," Van Steward said flatly.

"Change is coming. And it's coming fast. When our cathedrals burn openly in the city, our refuges defiled, and by our own people . . . the place to start is here, in Recityv. Now! Then, if some other threat besides our ignorance falls upon us, we will be ready, our house in order."

Roth straightened his cloak, slightly embarrassed for having lost so much of his composure. One last time, he surveyed the war room with its great maps and stately table and windows staring out on a day where men drilled and fires burned.

It had gone just as he'd hoped. Or at least just as he'd thought it would.

And he now knew where Van Steward would stand once Roth's plans got underway.

He nodded deferentially to Van Steward and made sure his boot heels clapped smartly as he strode now to take his audience with the Regent.

A Blade of Grass
of
Grass

INTRODUCTION

THERE'S A LOT TO do with language in The Vault of Heaven. You learn that the First Ones—aka the Framers, the Gods—used a certain language of their own to help fashion the world. It's a language that has intrinsic power. Cool idea, that. And one that's been around for centuries.

The thing that becomes interesting, I think, is how folks might try to use a language of power. To what end?

In *The Unremembered*, there's a scene with a widow in a small village. A widow that bears the scars of fire. I got a lot of email about her from readers. Her scene with one of my main characters seemed to strike a chord. Mostly with female readers, as it happens. They wanted to know more about her. Her backstory.

So did I.

That's why I wrote this one.

Truth is, I had most of it in my head. But as I got into the writing—as always happens—some interesting things surfaced. I got to explore the underpinnings of what might make a language of power work. And just as awesome was plumbing the emotional depth of a woman as strong as this one.

Because you haven't seen the last of her.

Not by a long shot.

And holy hell, when she finally finds her anger . . .

A Blade of Grass

THE FAMILIAR GLOW OF candlelight was the only companion allowed to Ja'Nene Lorashe in the private library of the League of Civility. At the canted surface of a semi-circular desk, she sat carefully examining passages from damaged texts. The words written on the old parchments proved hard to read by candlelight. The hour had grown late, but Ja'Nene worked on, believing she could finish in another week's time if she delayed taking her evening meals. Her diligence, though, hadn't only to do with meeting the self-imposed deadline. She thrilled at the assignment, which challenged her scrivener skills: weaving the several languages and disparate tracts into one treatise for the League, which had commissioned the work. The transcription progressed slowly, she admitted, not simply because of the dim light or lateness of the hour or even her weary eyes, but because the texts were mostly fragments: some marred by water; others with flaking ink; and many having simply faded to practically nothing. She wrote out another line on a fresh sheet, as she worked to collect many similar ideologies into a coherent statement that aligned itself with a recent treatise written for her by the League Ascendant himself.

Roth Staned. The leader of the League had authored this latest document, which he intended to become a creed, something his order had never formally declared. But he wanted any such creed to include a distillation of the diaries and wisdom of League men who had, for generations, led and counseled the order. It was daunting work, since besides the disrepair of so many of these various tracts, and notes, and diaries, their authors were from many nations and the texts written in many tongues.

Ja'Nene loved daunting work.

As she returned to the fragile, weathered documents, she came upon a section written in a looping backward scrawl. She'd never seen this language before, and the discovery was a welcome, unexpected delight. She bent close, scrutinizing the syllables of each word. As she examined the foreign words, she felt a chill creep over her skin,; and she thought again about the League's insistence that she perform this work alone, in this private, secluded study.

She read the passage again, hardly needing to track the words visually; after reading it once, she could see each letter and phrase in her mind. Not for the first time, she was grateful for her gift of precise memory. Now, she read aloud, forming the words deliberately as she worked her way through:

... malaetio som raaleth, corialuus lliusae falett soiuens maelicka ...

Halfway down the page, as she gently spoke the unfamiliar words, the candles guttered and died, plunging her into utter darkness. Something had stirred the air. She hadn't heard the door open, and she was alone. Her chill returned, and she hastily relit the candles.

The words were completely unfamiliar to her, and did not seem idiomatic of any language she knew. In addition, the page had been marred here and there by some stain or other. She hunched forward, scrutinizing each letter to find some clue as to its origin. The tongue was not a splinter dialect of Tilatian, as she had first guessed, nor a Mal idiom, another possibility she had considered. And it bore no likeness to either Dellian or Massonic speech. She was fluent in them all, and even when she'd read the passage aloud in various phonetic stylings of the words, she could find no correlation with known tongues.

Still, something *inside* the words seemed familiar. And the feeling that she should be able to recognize it nagged at her. She always felt a thrill when she discovered new language and meanings in her work, but this secrecy made her anxious. Not that it was without precedent for scriveners to work beyond the confines of their own halls and libraries—their services were used by many, including the Regent and her High Council—but since her years of training, Ja'Nene had never come upon a text written in a wholly unfamiliar tongue. And while she felt the excitement of discovering something new, her seclusion in the League library began to feel like confinement with a secret they did not want widely known.

Which led her to darker thoughts still. *Once I've completed the work, they will know I'm aware of this tract. What then? Will they think their secret is at risk?*

Scriveners took oaths of confidentiality, but the League had become more powerful and shown increasing volatility since Ascendant Staned had begun to lead—might they go to further lengths to ensure her silence. There were rumors . . .

She shot a look at the closed door, where a thin line of light from the hallway beyond shone upon the polished cedar floor. She then methodically surveyed the rest of the room—nothing but bookshelves, floor to ceiling; a cold hearth; two tables with unlit oil lamps; and several chairs attended by footstools. No windows.

"Breathe, Ja'Nene," she told herself, and shut her eyes to do just that. Imagination had ever been her hazard, even as it often proved her most valuable asset in deciphering cryptic or badly penned documents.

Lowering her gaze again, she focused once more on the parchment. After a moment, she repositioned it near the candle which rested on a flat ledge at the desk's high side. This time, though, she skipped the foreign words and picked up her reading where the document fell back into an idiom she knew, one most used near the shores of Calan Komalara, the great lakes of the Sotol Wastes.

> *. . . indecision is the disease of a weak mind. It is the first fruit of uncertainty and the last excuse of the coward. Better to cut away this disease than let it spread in the hearts of those who would otherwise stand firm. Therefore fear not the schism that tears you from your past. Let disunion be the goal if the reward is greater personal strength. Fill your morrow with hope, with an unfettered enthusiasm, for what you can bring to pass of your own accord . . .*

It read like a war sermon, like tidings of a dark gospel meant to embolden those who rode to battle. But the League did not participate in the military actions of her city, nor, so far as she knew, in such affairs of other nations. So, why were they asking Ja'Nene to incorporate this language in the creed she was helping create for the League of Civility?

She guessed that the answer to her question lay in the translation of the words there. Words that the League obviously hoped she could decipher given the context and the several documents they'd given her to scribe out this new creed.

Ja'Nene gathered the parchments into a pile and slipped them into the lock-box beneath the desk, all except the small sheet with the untranslatable text. That she slipped carefully into her satchel. She then gently dashed sand across her most recently written sheet, blew away the excess, and stoppered her ink. After she'd cleaned her stylus, she tucked her several well pens, as well as the ink, into a pouch. She took another deep breath to steady herself, then stood, keeping hold of the desk until she felt sure of her legs. Dousing a single candle, she used the other to light her way as she carried the finished pages to the door.

As she pulled the wide brass handle, a man stepped into the doorway, blocking her exit.

"Ascendant Staned?" She'd not seen the leader of the League since taking over this assignment from Miles, a fellow scrivener. The Ascendant had insisted on meeting her in person and offering to her the commission.

"Anais, you work late again," he observed, smiling pleasantly.

She resisted the impulse to clutch her satchel, which held the foreign language fragment, and handed him the finished pages. "It is quite a challenge you've put before me. I'm not sure I'll be able to translate it all."

"Come now," the Ascendant said with a light tone, "you're being modest. I'm told that aside from our friend Miles, there is not a finer Scrivener mind for languages."

She smiled at the compliment. "I won't deny that. But—" she stopped herself from speaking of the unknown language.

"Yes?" His brows rose expectantly.

"The trick is bringing it in line with the declarations you've made in your writing," she finished.

"Do you think me wrong-headed then?" he asked. "Perhaps my views depart too drastically from the past and we will not have a reconciliation of philosophies."

She heard a warning in his tone and tried to smile again. "It is only language," she replied, hoping her lie could not be detected. "I am not an author; I cannot create what is not there. But written words are like clay to me. I'll mold the proper form of them, I assure you. It may just take more time than I anticipated; I don't have all my usual resources at hand."

"I see," the man replied. "Then I must be patient, since I know how some view my fraternity, and so must take the precaution of having the work performed here." He raised his hands, indicating the League manor. "The documents you peruse are quite precious to me, to all Leaguemen."

"I understand." She felt anxious to be on her way. If she were caught trying to steal this bit of text . . .

"When will you finish, then?" the man asked, looking down at the pages she'd just delivered.

"Three or four weeks," she lied again.

"So long? I had thought your late hours would have the business done this week." The Ascendant looked up from the latest lines of the new League creed. "It appears you are progressing well."

"Thank you," she replied, and said no more.

The man then clasped his hands behind his back as would an orator preparing to speak. He leveled his powerful gaze on her and waited several breaths, allowing the silence to prepare them both for what he meant to say.

"As grateful as we are to have your keen gifts," he began, "You may count yourself equally fortunate to be helping us in this endeavor. Together we are distilling the wisdom of many into a way of thinking that will guide our way forward. Would you not agree?"

Ja'Nene returned the man's questioning stare. "With respect, Ascendant Staned, as I understand it, the philosophy of the League has been about unquestioned liberties for the common man. I think codifying all this," she pointed back toward the library, "into a new creed must be done carefully, so that you don't replicate the dominion you openly condemn."

As soon as she'd spoken, she regretted it. Just as with her mental recall of language on the page, she had always possessed the ability to see past the rhetoric and calling a thing what it was; it was that very skill that made her such a good scrivener. But it had often gotten her into trouble, since she sometimes didn't possess the restraint to refrain from using the skill when commenting to others.

She wished she could take back those words.

But the League leader only smiled in return. The smile conveyed anything but amusement. And he seemed to betray none of his true thoughts when he said, "We are lucky to have so balanced a scrivener hand at our behest."

With that, he escorted her to the door, and she heard the latch politely tick closed, as though the man had taken care not to suggest anger even in the shutting of the door. But all of it, from the discovery of the inscrutable text to the sound of a gently closed door, caused her to worry. She hurried into the night with the borrowed page of text.

C33O

MILES'S WIFE, RELANI, led Ja'Nene through a kitchen aromatic with fennel and parsley to the back bedroom, where Miles was laid up, sick. This came as no surprise; it was the reason for her current assignment. When he had taken ill, he knew the only other scribbler with the languages background for this commission was Ja'Nene. But today, her colleague . . . his skin had gone pale as goat's milk.

She quickly surveyed the room—a matter of habit—as she drew near her elderly colleague.

"Ah, a linguist, just what every sick man needs. Come in." The effort to talk produced a coughing spasm that sent him reaching for the cup of water at his bed-table.

She sat facing him, and Relani withdrew. "How are you, Miles?"

"Oh my, you're not going to go through the customary greetings are you? I haven't the voice for it. You know how I am. Look at me." He smiled and wiped his lips with the blanket that lay across his chest.

"Fair enough. You look awful. What do the healers say, though? What has you down?" Ja'Nene began to steal glances around the room, not sure what she might be looking for.

"I'm down here," Miles said, and his voice then became quite serious. "Look at me, Anais Ja'Nene."

"Anais? You're delirious," she said, smiling. But when Miles spoke again the humor fell away quickly.

"I've been sick for three weeks, Ja'Nene, and this is the first time you have come to see me." He paused and drew several panting breaths. "We are friends, but that is not why you came here tonight, is it?

She stared at him. She wished she could say that friendship alone had brought her here. Suddenly, she did not wish to speak about any of it. But his eyes invited her to share the truth, and with that invitation, she opened her satchel and handed him the foreign passage. As he looked it over, she recited the untranslated words from memory, recalling their letters and shapes and offering the most common sounds for each, spoken in the idiom of the lake shores in the Sotol Wastes.

She couldn't be sure, but she thought she heard the rustling of loose pages, as though the gentlest of winds had stirred a bed of scrolls Miles kept in the corner. Looking briefly there, she saw a book with a cracked binding, its cover sitting slightly separated and askew from the pages within. She had only glanced there before, and did not remember seeing the broken binding. Had it been rent just now?

She kept on, and when she finished, the two shared a long, searching look. She thought her friend had grown paler still. His breathing had become more shallow, and sweat stood out on his brow and cheeks.

"Have you translated it?" her fellow scrivener finally asked, his eyes guarded.

She shook her head. "Parts of the words seem familiar, but I lose them inside pairings that make no sense to me. And while the sound of it spoken feels natural, even lyrical, somehow I sense the words are more *curse than courtesy*." She stopped after using the old scrivener adage, reluctant to ask him if he'd succeeded in translating the difficult passage.

Seeming to know her mind, he said, "I could not decipher the words either. Then I grew sick, and had to find a replacement." He tapped her knee. "I should have asked Midge instead of you."

They both laughed at that. Midge Taloot stalked the scrivener halls and studies, always seeming to find an insult for those he happened upon. Usually, he criticized the work of his fellow scriveners —the old man read *everything* his fellows produced, and did so with amazing speed—and if there wasn't a handy craft-related barb to fling, he was just as apt to comment on your appearance, even though his own wattled neck and vein-ridden nose made him quite the sight.

Miles's laughter turned to a wet cough, and he dabbed blood from his lips and tongue with a rag he'd apparently used previously to do the same.

"What's going on, Miles?"

Her long-time friend showed a weary, defeated smile. "I'm dying, Ja'Nene. A few days more, I think."

Rubbing at the blood-soaked rag, her friend spoke thoughtfully. "It's not the chest fever. That's what the healers say it is. But I think I know the difference. No, Ja'Nene, this was . . . *intentional*."

Her heart thumped hard at the suggestion. "How? Why?" She looked from Miles hands, which were still worrying at the blood-rag, to his face again. "Who?"

He offered a wan smile. "Maybe it's just the desire of an old scrivener to assign value to his life. Couldn't be that I just came down sick, could it." He laughed; coughed again. "But it feels like poison, lass. Not that a man can know such a thing for certain, since he'd only likely ever feel it once, eh?" He smiled at his own dark logic. "Still, that's the sense I get of it. And why? Who? I can only speculate, but if it hasn't to do with that damned creed I'll go to my earth a misjudging fool." He raised the parchment with trembling fingers, then set it on his bed table.

She put her hands over Miles's own, to calm them. "You were only doing what they asked. What reason would they have to do this?"

"A very good question," he replied. "But here's the crux of the matter, and pay you mind. I'm not necessarily saying that someone put tincture in something I ate or drank—"

"What then?" she interjected.

"I don't know what this foreign passage says, lass. But unless I am truly gone in the mind, something in those words has effects beyond the page. Even without comprehending their meaning, the words have laid hold of me." He offered another wan smile. "I haven't your ability of recall, but I nevertheless cannot forget the shape and sound of those words." Her friend lifted his bloody rag and made a bad job of wiping his lips. Covering his mouth, he began to cry.

"I will bring Raelas," Ja'Nene said, and stood to go out to do it right then. Her husband was Sheason; he could help her friend.

Miles held her hand firmly, and drew her back to his bedside. He shook his head as he brought his sobs under control. "I wouldn't put his life at odds with the Civilization Order; he would soon wind up lying next to me in his own earth for rendering the Will. No Sheason, lass. Understand, I don't despair over my own life."

Her friend raised weary eyes to her own. "But I must beg your forgiveness, Ja'Nene." His eyes then became glassy again with un-shed tears. "I knew better. Though I couldn't be sure of any of it.

When I first felt ill, and left my contract with the League—when I ask you to stand in for me—I could sense something. I think now it was my own bookish pride that prevented me from seeing the ties between the transcription and my sudden ailment." He squeezed her hand, and glanced sideways at the old parchment. "You see. I allowed you to go in my place . . . I am so sorry, lass. Please forgive me."

She leaned in and hugged the old scrivener close. She whispered in his ear, "I am fine. Perhaps it is your illness that suggests these connections, trying to make sense of what is happening to you. Regardless, you must think no more of it. I hold no ill feelings toward you."

The old man's body relaxed beneath her, as if freed from the burden of some weight. She drew slightly back, pausing to smile at him. He kissed her gently on the cheek. She could feel the wetness of blood there, but did not move to wipe it away.

She sat fully upright in and, in a brighter tone said, "I think you are on the mend."

Miles ignored her attempt at optimism. "You've been delivering your work each day, I assume."

She nodded. "Why?"

His eyes showed a new kind of worry. "That you've come here with these questions will also mean that the League is aware of your exact place in the transcriptions. I know of it, because I look ahead. That's my way. You, on the other hand, are one to start at the beginning and proceed methodically through the text."

Ja'Nene recalled the brief exchange she'd had just an hour ago with the Ascendant as she prepared to leave. *It appears you are progressing well . . . We are lucky to have so balanced a scrivener hand at our behest.*

"You think I'm in danger," she surmised.

"As you say, I'm ill. Could be that I'm not thinking clearly. But the longer I lay here . . . I think there are things in those texts that the employer will not publish when he releases his new creed; and this bit of language—" he motioned to the borrowed language fragment "—is likely one of them. And I don't trust his comfort with someone outside the League knowing the details of what remains hidden."

"Then he must already know what the passage says," Ja'Nene reasoned. "Why would he ask us to translate something he already understands?"

Miles shook his head, his brow furrowing in concentration. "I'm fairly certain Roth doesn't know what the words say. Nor that they may hold any intrinsic power. It's just not in him to believe the old ways."

Ja'Nene silently found that in this regard, at least, she agreed with the Ascendant—language had power, but not the way people believed the conceiver's tongue did, if such a tongue existed at all.

"But," Miles continued, "I get the feeling that the man has a general sense of the passage. Its topic, if you understand me. Could be that he wishes to bolster his creed by showing that even sacred text supports the League's philosophies."

She listened to these possible explanations, looking for flaws in the logic. "How would Roth even know about such a text? How would he come by it?"

"Again, lass, I think the man pursues a kind of unified wisdom to create his creed. And if he can show that the very evidence, the old words, that others would use to contend with him can actually reinforce his position . . . Plus, I spent a full turn of the moon in that library; and in my time there, I saw strange men. Outlanders, Ja'Nene, whose dialects I could not name."

The old scrivener began to cough, choking a bit on the blood he brought up from his lungs. Ja'Nene helped him sit up to better clear his throat—some of the blood he produced this time had begun to thicken.

"I won't hear any more argument," she said. "Raelas and I will return tonight when the streets are empty. He will see to your health."

This time, Miles did not argue, and lay back, grimacing with the effort.

She reached to collect the foreign text fragment. Her colleague weakly caught her wrist. "Leave it," he said. "I've nothing but time lying here. Perhaps I can help you decipher this after all."

"Are you sure?" she asked. "What if you are correct about it possessing some inherent—"

"I'm sure," he said, his tone firm, even with his weakened voice.

Ja'Nene gave her friend a quick kiss on the forehead and stood up. When she reached the street, her mind racing ahead to her husband, a member of the Order of Sheason, she suddenly thought she knew where she'd seen some of the phonemes and phonic couplings in the foreign passage she'd come upon tonight.

A few steps beyond the house, she broke into a dead run.

CȝEↃ

SHE BURST THROUGH THE door and threw it shut behind her. Raelas looked up in surprise, but she ignored his inquiring look, and went immediately to her writing table. Not bothering to sit, she grabbed a fresh sheet of parchment. Leaning over the table, she took hold of a stylus, dipped it in the standing ink well, and steadied herself. She must form the words precisely as she'd seen them; variations in the written shape of a single letter suggested colorings to the sound of the word. She pictured them in her head, and set to writing.

As she meticulously recreated the foreign words, Raelas drew up beside her, silently watching her work. She'd always loved about him that he knew as well when not to speak as when to be heard. Eight times she returned her pen to the well to craft the lines. When she'd finished, they were, to her memory, as accurate a recreation as was possible. She'd even taken care to recreate thin or nearly absent words and letters as they'd appeared in the marred text she'd seen early that evening in the League library.

She did not sand the ink, nor even blow it dry. She simply waited, looking down at the words, suddenly feeling as though she'd invited a stranger into their home.

Ja'Nene did not look away from the transcription when she asked, "Do you recognize it?"

Raelas continued to study the lines with her for several moments before answering. She heard him shaking his head before he said, "No."

"Look *inside* the words." She pointed with her stylus, taking care not to touch the page. Throughout the passage she indicated several sonant pairings, some combined with sibilants in a repeated pattern.

A closed-lip sound came from deep in Raelas's throat—his sound of thoughtful concern.

"Is this what I think it is?" she asked.

"It looks like it." He bent so close to the parchment, she feared he might smudge the ink with his nose. "It's not precisely as I've seen it written in the vestige texts I've studied, but it's too close to ignore the similarities. Where did you get this?"

She took him by the arm and drew him up to face her. "It's part of the transcription I'm doing for the League."

Raelas's thoughtful concern hastened toward real worry. "I don't understand. The League repudiates the idea of the covenant tongue. It's one of the grievances they used to justify the Civilization Order against my own fraternity. Do you realize what this could mean?"

"I didn't bring this to you as grounds to challenge the League." Ja'Nene turned and began to pace, still seeing in her mind the words she'd just penned. "I need to decipher their meaning, Raelas. I need your help getting at the meaning of the diphthongs and smaller parts of the words. You had to study these to become Sheason."

She watched him draw an oil lamp closer to provide more light as he pored over the words again. After several moments, he began to shake his head. "They're similar, but it's as though they've come through several translations, and small errors or changes have been introduced over time, obscuring their origins. I could guess, but you know that where this kind of language is concerned, precision is everything."

Ja'Nene felt a rush of understanding. She quickly stepped back to the writing table and looked with Raelas at the words on the parchment. "Perhaps you are right. Perhaps they've been recopied so many times that they are a hairs breadth different from where they began." She shut her eyes. "Or perhaps the changes were introduced . . . *intentionally*."

"A shading of the language that subtle would take an expert hand. And reproducing it an equal, maybe greater, skill." He looked at her, understanding dawning in his own face. "Ja'Nene, you can't go back. Whatever the passage actually says, whether it's an error in transcription or the art of a gifted linguist, it can come to no good."

Then everything crystallized in her mind, and she was reluctant to say what she thought out loud. Still, she could find no other conclusion, and it chilled her. "They're euonym fragments, aren't they, Raelas? Somehow the League has found a portion of the conceiver's tongue, and wishes to seal its creed with these words."

The man she loved shook his head, whether in disbelief or shock she could not say. Euonyms. The very names of things. The proof of a lexical reality that had power to influence matter. The Philosophy of Language held that some words possessed latent power that could be realized if properly expressed. Linguistic theorists had for ages suggested that the true name of a thing was part of the matter of which it was constituted. More recent theory had taken this notion several steps further, positing that the language had potency separate from the matter. The proof of this would be that misspellings and mispronunciations could have effect on the natural world as surely as did the accurate use of any given euonym.

The oldest religions and children's rhymes carried forward this idea in the premise that the world had been founded by use of a pure language that commanded the elements—the conceiver's tongue. And against the threat of yet other fables, like those told of the Quiet races, the nations of the east had for generations set many of its most gifted scriveners to the task of piecing together this legendary language. Many thought it a fool's pursuit; but libraries like the one at Qum'rahm'se nonetheless sought this lexicon. Many deemed it a worthwhile intellectual pursuit to find a vernacular so pure or natural that it would become a true common tongue, something all could speak and understand without having to relearn another language.

Ja'Nene had realized, as she offered Miles the healing assistance of her Sheason husband, that the Order was required to study and master the use of words thought to belong to this oldest of tongues. But it had never been clear to her that the words Raelas had learned possessed any intrinsic power or authority. It seemed more akin to what her guild called the Discipline of Ideology, the use of ideas to focus study and critical thought. The subject had been the source of many spirited debates between her and Raelas, most of which usually ended with her feeling vindicated.

As she thought again of Miles, she felt less sure.

Raelas interrupted her stream of thoughts. "It may be that this is ceremonial on their part. Perhaps it is the Ascendant playing politics, including a passage of an old tract to suggest his willingness to compromise with those who are suspicious of the League, those who still hold to old traditions."

But she heard him only distantly. In her mind she reviewed the words again and again, trying to discern their origin. She'd come to believe that decrypting the seminal meaning of these etymons would lead her to understand the true meaning behind the creed she'd been asked to distill from so many texts.

Raelas had again turned to examine the parchment. She moved through possible cognates of the letter pairings from other languages, using the oldest tongues she'd mastered: oiue, aeli, lliu, aa.

The deeper she delved into the various sounds these diphthongs could produce the closer she felt herself cycling to the *feeling* of a word.

Their small home grew barrow quiet, as they each concentrated on these word parts, ignoring the full set of letters the way a miner chips past rock and soil to find pure ore.

Sometime later—she did not know how long—they found themselves staring at one another in a moment of awful epiphany. There seemed to be a nomenclature to these blocks of text; vowel couplings and a family of sounds that shared an intention after all:

With grave concern, she began to find a kind of etymology: "Uncouple, rend . . ."

"Sunder, diverge, dissolve," Raelas added.

She nodded. "Discriminate, alienate . . ."

"Alone," he said.

It took her a moment to find the end of it, but when she did, she felt her heart pounding in her chest. "Annihilate."

"They can't mean this." Raelas tapped the page on the desk behind him. "Not even the League. The Ascendant is dogged and uncompromising, but he's not violent."

Ja'Nene considered it. "Do any of us understand the full meaning of the words we use? Most have no sense of where they came from or what they may have once meant. They may know only that the words generally connote separating oneself from a dependency on someone or something. That would be consistent with their doctrine of self-reliance and self-improvement."

"Or they may have guessed at its deeper meanings," Raelas countered. "Whether purposeful or by accident, these words could imbue their creed with more than a political and philosophical foundation, Ja'Nene. You really can't go back there. And I must share this threat with my own order."

A deeper fear took hold of her. "The creed will add some language, but mostly it is meant to distill the thought of several prior tracts . . . I believe the League is already sworn to these words, even if their full meaning is yet hidden from them."

"Let's go," Raelas said.

He extended a hand to her, but before she could take it, there came a knock at the door. His brows went up in question, and he turned to see who was calling.

Ja'Nene felt coldness spread in the pit of her stomach as the door swept open and she saw four Leaguemen standing there.

"May we come in?" the lead man asked, a hint of predatory smile on his lips.

Raelas did not move. "It's late, and we're about to take supper. Can we speak tomorrow?"

"I'm afraid not, Sheason." The man looked past her husband directly at Ja'Nene. "We must speak now."

Reluctantly, he stepped back, admitting them. When he'd closed the door, he came around to stand between her and their four visitors. "What is this about?"

The man simply looked at her. "Would you like to tell him?"

There was no point in denying that she'd taken the text. But she also had no reason to lie. "The text is unknown to me. I've asked the scrivener originally assigned to the commission to help me translate it."

"I see," said the Leagueman, looking around their home with a tad of condescension. "Why did you not tell us of this?"

"My apologies. It is rather embarrassing that I needed help. It's not something I wished to announce." This *was* a lie—something she typically did badly—and she stole a look at Raelas, whose gaze remained fixed on their visitors.

The Leagueman made a sound of disbelief deep in his throat. "Well, regardless of that being true or not, we must ask that for the remainder of your commission you stay at the manor with us."

"No," Raelas said. "She will remain with me. And before another scrivener returns to the work, we will have some questions answered."

The other paused, having paced near her writing table, and stared down at her reproduction of the foreign passage. He picked it up and held it out like a bit of incriminating evidence. "How many copies of this have you made, Scrivener?"

"Just the one you hold," she replied, as the feeling in the room tightened. "I came upon the passage today. I'm trying to work it through."

The man nodded as one does when he's convinced another is lying. He folded the parchment and tucked it inside his shirt. "I won't ask again," he said. "We will go now."

The man and one of his companions advanced toward Ja'Nene.

Panic struck her, and she bolted for the rear door. The two Leagueman were fast upon her; and she saw the other two men seize Raelas, in the same moment.

"Ja'Nene!" Raelas cried, and managed to pull free.

He immediately drew his hands up in sweeping arcs, rendering the Will, slamming to the floor the two Leaguemen holding him. Leaping over them, he came for her, but pulled up short when a knife's edge touched her throat.

"That's far enough, Sheason."

She could feel the man's hot breath on her ear as he spoke. It smelled of parsley and fennel. She felt a warm drop of water run down her neck, and realized the blade had cut her skin, drawing blood.

The Leagueman backed away, pulling her further from Raelas. "Your woman has lost our confidence. We'll have to hold her for a while."

"On what authority?" Raelas challenged.

"Tread carefully, Sheason. We have witnessed your use of the Will here. We could just as easily take you into custody for violating the Civilization Order. But I might be convinced to overlook it this once."

"You mean if I let you leave here with my wife, whose crime is nothing more than translating your silly creed?" Raelas replied, incredulous, and began to shake his head.

The Leagueman's grip on her tightened. She could see both fear and anger in her husband's face. Her heart pounded. She believed if she were taken from her home now, she would never see Raelas again. And with the thought, she also realized where she'd smelled parsley and fennel early that very evening: Miles. This bastard had paused long enough at her fellow scrivener's home to scoop some stew into his maw before coming here.

Are you alive, Miles?

"A Sheason calls our creed 'silly.' You are a fool of many hats to say it."

Raelas then shared a look with Ja'Nene: *Be ready.*

A moment later, the Leagueman's knife pulled away from her throat. She glanced and saw her husband's palm slightly raised as he drew on the Will again. She wasted no time and ducked out of the way. Just as she got clear, one of the first Leagueman, who had recovered from his violent collision with the wall, tackled Raelas, driving him to the floor.

Raelas's rendering died, and behind her the Leagueman grunted as one might when heaving something heavy. As she turned to meet him, the oil lamp struck her face and shattered, splashing oil on her brow and cheek. The flame lit the oil, and her skin began to grow hot. She could smell burning hair and her left eye clouded over in an instant.

She panicked, and raced past the Leaguemen into the street, only able to think of finding a water trough to douse the flames. Twice, she tried to wipe away the oil and fire, succeeding only in spreading the damage.

Running blindly down the street, it seemed a very long time before she ducked down a narrow alley and found a trough. She dunked her head in the cool water that smelled of horseflesh and straw.

She then collapsed to the muddy ground, able to focus on nothing but the pain in her skin, which felt as though it was yet afire. Her hands had likewise burned, but not so badly, and she'd lost the use of one eye.

Distantly, she heard more commotion. *Raelas?*

Boots pounded the street, and she tucked herself up beneath a nearby boardwalk until the sound of frantic movement and the cries of the Leaguemen to one another faded completely.

Then she tried to stand, but was too weak from shock. So she had to crawl back toward her house, just able to keep herself from crying.

Though when she finally crept back through the door into the silence of her home, she could no longer hold back her sobs, and her grief came on full. Raelas lay against the wall, blood spreading in a pool beneath his head. And as painful as it was to see him lie there unmoving, his eyes glassy with a thousand-league stare, she began to realize that she had lost more than his mortal companionship. She couldn't put a name to it at first, despite all her scrivener training.

When she reached her love and gently kissed his forehead, it finally came on her: *detraehnimuus*.

An epithet formed of many of the sonant pairings she'd found in the League's foreign text. A word she knew belonged to that portion of the lost tongue Raelas's order studied in their training. A word that had less a mortal connotation, and more one of lasting consequence. It had no equivalent in extant languages; the closest was: *Separation*.

But that was insufficient. It did not fully convey the feeling. There was, intrinsic to its sound, a meaning she couldn't at this moment fully appreciate. But she sensed it. And her despair deepened well beyond what she felt about the mortal years with Raelas that were now forfeit.

She buried the un-ruined side of her face in her husband's chest and wept.

C3𝔅

THE WIND BIT AT the still tender flesh of her burned cheek and brow. Clouds rolled low not far above her and her Sheason companion, who had arrived not long after she returned to the house, and escorted Ja'Nene promptly from the city; the League would not have waited long before they resumed their search for her. For a week she and the Sheason had traveled westward, sharing silence, keeping private thoughts. For her part, she felt a growing sense of aloneness that seemed larger than the death of her beloved. On the countenance of her escort, she saw alternating expressions of sadness and concern.

In the half-light of dusk, they stood where the alder woods thinned. They'd recently traveled through the dense forest, the Sheason stopping as if unwilling to go further. To the side of the narrow path, the horses nosed through dry grass, seeking something green. Ja'Nene drew her cloak around her arms to ward off the chill of twilight. The Sheason beside her pointed ahead. Far down the widening path, a small collection of huts seemed to huddle together against a bruised sky, which threatened rain.

"You will find the company of widows here," he explained.

"Safe from the League," she added, understanding at least part of the intent of bringing her to this place.

The other nodded. "It is unknown to them."

"It appears desolate," she said, looking around at the bare limbs and leafless scrub and dead grasses.

To this, her guide said nothing. It seemed he'd completed his task, desired to say no more, nor to enter the village ahead.

She then had a despairing thought, one that touched her profoundly. *I will never leave this place.* There seemed a certainty in it. Without thinking, she hurried over near the horses, and began to search the ground with them. It took her some time, but she finally found what she sought—a few blades of live grass. She plucked and lifted them to study. The soft green eased her heart, if only a little.

She took the reins of her mount and started toward this widow's village with room for but two thoughts in her mind. The one warring with the other.

Detraehnimuus . . . separation.

And the poignancy of the only life she could seem to find in his place: her blades of grass.

THE
GREAT DEFENSE
OF
LAYOSAH

INTRODUCTION

FIFTEEN YEARS AGO, when I wrote *The Unremembered*, I knew one day I'd write this story. I also dreaded it a bit.

In the book, you get a retelling of part of the story from a trouper boy. I like how that came out. But it never had the full emotional weight of the story in my head. And I didn't feel like I could take the room in the novel to write it all out.

So, I punted.

Fast forward a lot of years. I got a book contract from Tor. They were going to publish my fantasy series. And as a way to start sharing the world I'd created, we thought a few short stories might make sense.

And I began to panic.

Because I knew I had to write this story.

At one point, I was in the Barnes & Noble in Bellevue, Washington, wandering around, pretending to look at books. Really, I was obsessing about this story. And more specifically, the ending. I had a conflict running right the hell down my spine. Made me shiver. I finally sat in one of their comfy chairs and called my editor. It was pretty late for him. To his credit, he understood my feelings, and we talked a while.

It didn't help me decide which way to go, but it made me slightly more confident that I wasn't a whack job. I mean, who would fret this much over a story decision?

Ultimately, I made my decision and wrote the story. I believe I made the right call. But I can still see the other ending. Haunts me some.

This might be my favorite story in this collection. I have tons of respect for Layosah. Like Efram from "Sacrifice of the First Sheason," my thought is that we need more Layosahs in this world.

She's one hell of a woman.

THE GREAT DEFENSE
OF
LAYOSAH

L AYOSAH REYAL SAT AT her kitchen table across from the two
visitors, and ignored them. In her arms, her baby started to
cry. She whispered softly to Audra to soothe her, as the two soldiers
from the Recityv army patiently waited. The closer man balled a
fist, his leather glove creaking in the stillness. Layosah had noticed
her callers' clean cloaks and polished blades when they entered her
home—these were no men-at-arms, but a special envoy. She knew
it to be true when she finally looked up from Audra and saw the
look in their eyes. That, and the carefully bound package the second
man held in almost ceremonial fashion.

"Anais Layosah Reyal . . ." The first soldier paused, his gaze gentle
and kind. She was already nodding. "Anais Layosah," he started
again, softer, "by custom we come to honor your son's sacrifice in
the defense of his nation, his people, his brothers . . . and his family."
The young soldier looked down at Audra. "We will mourn with you."

The empty ache spread in her stomach again, as it had before.
She began to tremble. The second soldier quickly rose and lit the
kitchen hearth behind her. Neither spoke until more light and
warmth came to the small kitchen—a place once filled with the

167

voices of her family raised over endfast smells of fried root and morning honey bread.

The silence gave Layosah time to travel back through memory, where she caught glimpses of smiles and laughter and her husband Eddock's strong but careful touch—it had been his gentleness that had convinced her to accept his proposal to wed. The first soldier—he looked so young, hardly older than . . . she mustn't think that—cleared his throat, breaking the spell of her reverie, and drew her back to the dreadful reality of the present.

He began to speak. "Anais Layosah, some weeks ago, at the far end of the kingdom of Nallan, General Stallworth's army was beset by legions out of the Bourne. They came unexpectedly, a great dark army three times the size of the one we were already fighting. Weary men took up their blades and met the Quiet with valor, but many . . . most . . . were lost."

Tears for her lost son began to fall hot and silent down Layosah's cheeks. As the young soldier spoke, she imagined her son Aelon, barely eighteen, fighting, struggling, up to his last breath.

Six, she thought. *I've lost six.*

Her eldest boy, Maalen, had gone first. He and Eddock had joined the ranks of General Stallworth's army together. Eddock had returned from that first march alone. A year later, Toele, her next boy. And two years on from that, Simick. Another great march—three years after Simick had been laid down—had sent both her beloved and his younger brother, Ren, north through the Wynstout Dominion; this time, neither returned.

The law required healthy men who reached the age of eighteen and had passed their Change into accountability to take up the crimson banner of Recityv and fight in this endless war.

So it was that all her older sons had gone. And Eddock was gone, leaving her alone and pregnant with a child whose face her father would never see, a child whose surprise arrival had brought some happiness to her when her heart grieved for the children she had already lost. She looked down at Audra. "Six," she whispered to the babe, then took a shuddering breath, the full force of her grief descending upon her.

In her sorrow, and looking at the child in her arms, she recalled becoming pregnant for the first time, and Eddock's joy over the news.

"I must buy milk this time," she had said.

Her husband had frowned. "Hate the taste of it. Don't waste the coin."

"It's not for you," Layosah told him, a hint of something more in her voice.

He looked up from the blade grip he sat lashing. "We don't have money for milk . . . why milk?" he asked, understanding beginning to bloom in his face—milk was said to be the best nourishment for a mother with child.

"His name will be Maalen," Layosah said. "Your father's name. And if he's half as stubborn as you are, I swear I will—"

But she never finished her oath, as Eddock stood, pulled her close, and put his mouth on hers. After a long kiss, he had drawn back and given her a playfully mocking smile. "Milk?"

Forever after, the sight or smell of it had reminded her of that first happiness over the beginnings of their family.

The messenger had continued to speak as she had remembered that moment, remembered her beloved and *all* her sons whose blood had been shed in this never-ending war against the Bourne.

These purveyors of ill news came weekly back to Recityv, into the homes of the fallen, to honor their memory and sacrifice by making a full accounting of how they had fought . . . and died.

"Yours is a grim task," she said softly, interrupting the young soldier.

He showed her a forlorn smile. "Yes, Anais, a grim labor. But for your ears alone . . . I would rather someone else convey these tidings so that I could see *my* sword stained and nicked." The young man slowly ran a hand down his scabbard. "It is a shame to wear a merely ceremonial blade."

"Your mother may not think so," Layosah replied.

The second soldier, an older man—giving her the sense that, of the two, the younger had the greater gift for words—stepped around the table, and knelt. He drew forth the long, wrapped parcel he'd been so protectively holding, and held it out to her on open palms.

Layosah looked first at the bearer, then at the gift. No secret was this. Neatly wrapped in fine brushed leathers would be her Aelon's sword and some of his personal effects, too. She looked at it for a moment before great uncontrollable sobs racked her body.. Her heart ached yet again when she turned weeping eyes to the left, where the wall had been fixed with pegs, upon which five other swords now rested—the markers of her dead sons and her beloved.

In her anguish, she held Audra close, fearful that her child would one day be sitting in her own home, in her own kitchen, receiving such news. It was a legacy the women of Recityv had shared for generations. She had too many friends who had likewise lost their sons, and who were now little more than mothers whose wombs manufactured soldiers to go and die in faraway places; mothers whose wombs created daughters who grew only, it seemed, to suffer as their mothers suffered, to hear the same dark tidings.

We are the wombs of war, she thought, as she so often had. In fact, many women—now childless by virtue of this war—had formed a sisterhood in Recityv. Until this moment, they'd mostly comforted one another when news came of fallen loved ones. Until this moment, they'd found a hard-won pride in being "wombs of war." Until this moment, which, of all the moments that had come before, struck her differently... because her last child, like her, would bear life unto death, would be left behind to grieve as she did now.

No more. I will not give Recityv another daughter for its war.

She looked down at Audra. *You will not be a womb of war. Even if I must...* But she left that thought unfinished.

☙

LAYOSAH HAD NOT HUNG Aelon's sword on her wall with all the others. It was as grim a task as that given to the messenger whose departure just hours ago she could not recall. He'd likely slipped out during the long hours of her grief after the news of her son's death and his blade had been delivered; no doubt the young solider had other calls to make. Instead, she now carried the sword, still wrapped as it had come, in one arm, Audra cradled in the other. She bustled through the streets of Recityv, passing traders and alley barkers and lines of army recruits being walked by men in Recityv crimson toward the city garrison and training yards. She would have followed one of these, had she not known the way by heart.

Five times before she had walked this exact route. Except today her visit was not to bid a loved one farewell, nor to stand at the garrison gate and look on mournfully as the "Parade of the Fallen"—as the people called it—made its slow procession down the concourse. No, not that. Not today.

She paid no heed to the guards standing attendance on either side of the garrison entrance. She moved fast and focused on the great building at the far end of the long courtyard. There, she knew, the general and his officers' cabinet planned and strategized and consigned men to death.

Before she could pass the gate, however, two men were abruptly in her path. "You aren't allowed—"

She shoved the wrapped blade into their faces. "This is my permission, young man. Or will you deny entry to a mother who has sent six to their final earth defending our people." She poked his chest where his tabard was emblazoned with the Recityv sigil—a tree with roots as deep as its limbs stretched high.

The two guards shared a look.

"Come with me then, and see that I make no trouble. That satisfy you?" Layosah got moving around them.

One of the guards fell in on her left and a step behind. Together they briskly walked the parade route toward the quarters of General Stallworth himself.

By the Sky I'll see this done!

As they traversed the long, wide street, she held the thought that many young men had passed this way, marching in time to military drums or the call of their captains; and that many of those—including all the men of her family—would never set down another boot on these cobblestones.

Layosah bent her shoulders forward, and drove her aching legs harder toward this man whose war had left her nearly childless. At the high double doors, boldly graven with the Recityv sigil, two more men-at-arms stepped into her path, barring her. She nearly said something, but then her escort raised a hand. They gave him a deferential look and stood aside.

In the crisp morning air she boldly strode past them. Her escort quickly got ahead of her and led her through the door and beneath the high ceiling of a spartan receiving room. They angled immediately right, the young gate guard signaling with his hand to forestall yet another sentry's attempt to block them from entering this last chamber.

Audra fussed a bit. Layosah bent her head toward the babe and spoke soothingly: "Be still, my dear. We are about to do some denouncing."

She kissed her child's forehead, still clutching tight the sword of her dead son, and followed her escort into the war room.

Here the ceiling rose every bit as high as that of the entry hall—twenty strides, she guessed. On the rear and side walls, from corner to corner, great maps had been painted in fine detail. In the middle of the room, beneath brightly shining braziers, stood a large table cluttered with yet more maps laid flat, upon which figurines of men and horses were positioned in various places that Layosah could tell represented lands far from Recityv.

In the air hung an acrid odor—men long without a bath, perhaps having slept little, slaving over their strategies and the miniature statues that represented men sent to war. A few of these soldiers, fitted in uniforms of crimson and white, stood together in corners, speaking in hushed tones. She wondered if they spoke reverently of the men whose deaths came as a result of their orders. Others stood near the maps on the walls or on the table, studying, scrutinizing the terrain and the figurines as if the inanimate things might move of their own accord.

Layosah took it all in with a glance, then headed for General Stallworth, a man she'd met before—he'd visited her himself after Ren had been killed. Her swift movement in the war room, the clap of her shoes, or some other noise brought the man's attention to her while she was yet several strides away. The expression on his face made it clear that he remembered her, and that he knew why she had come.

As she drew near, he turned toward her.

"Stallworth," she began, dispensing with his title, "you have claimed now six of my family with your failed plans. Your maps and war councillors do you no good." She threw Aelon's sword upon the table, where it clanked and stirred the maps, knocking over dozens of the figurines.

"I had the report given to me personally," Stallworth replied. "He was a valiant young man. Though I know the honor of his sacrifice does you little comfort."

As the general spoke, another man wearing a long grey cloak came up beside him. Layosah noted the sigil of the Order of Sheason on a chain around his neck.

"Six," she repeated. "A husband and five sons. My womb has been your weapon, and you use it badly."

Stallworth reached out a hand to gently touch her arm in consolation. She slapped it away. "I do not seek your sympathy or your pity. I want to know how you are going to end this. Because by my Skies, I will not let the only child left to me become another supplier of soldiers. You must bring an end to it. Tell me. Tell me how you are going to do it, Stallworth. Tell me the women of this city are not conceiving another generation of sons whose mothers will outlive them, and daughters whose inheritance will be childlessness and loss."

The general stood silent for a long time. The Sheason beside him looked at Audra.

Layosah shook her head in disgust. As she did so, at the edge of her vision, she caught sight of something she hadn't noticed before. She turned, leaning out over the table and the map. With an unsteady hand she reached out and took up one of the small figurines. Drawing it near, she inspected it, her heart beginning to race—not for the representation of the beastly Bar'dyn, creatures of nightmare from the distant Bourne, but because of the sight of the huge number of Bar'dyn figurines she'd inadvertently knocked over when she threw down her son's blade.

Her pulse quickened further at what she saw next. Even as she looked out across the map, several of the figures representing Stallworth's forces simply vanished. She stared, dumbfounded, with an awful feeling in the pit of her stomach.

For several moments, she could find no words, only pointing. Then, finally, she looked up at General Stallworth, holding the miniature Bar'dyn out toward him. "What does this mean?"

Stallworth drew a long breath, meeting her gaze. "The Quiet descends from the Bourne in numbers . . . beyond what we could have imagined. And it is not just Bar'dyn, but strange creatures unlike anything we have ever seen. And so many. The men stand firm." He paused, his features tightening. "But they are as lambs to the slaughter. When their figures fade from our table . . ."

She imagined Aelon standing, helpless on some distant plain, watching a huge force advancing toward him, knowing he would die. "And here, you simply watch a token disappear. . . ."

Layosah clenched the figure of the Bar'dyn in her fist, feeling the jab of its edges in her palm. "What are you going to do about it?" she demanded. "I hear defeat in your voice. Either discover the way to victory—you and all your cronies here—or get into your saddle and go yourself to stand with the men you commit to die beneath this wave of Quietgiven." She stepped close to him, feeling his breath on her nose as she looked up at him. "Because by all that lives, I will not stand idle knowing that the blood of my men was spilt for nothing. Someone must take action!"

To her surprise, the Sheason beside Stallworth nodded.

The general's hard gaze softened. "It is a war bigger than Recityv, Anais Reyal. Bigger than men. We fight it the best we can—"

"Then that is not good enough!" Her shout brought cries from her child, but she did not relent. "Your war has lasted generations, Stallworth. Generals before you failed. Now you fail—"

"Of course we fail!" His eyes hardened. "We fight alone! We've entreated other realms to join us, and yet we have not one ally in this war. Some won't join us for fear of reprisal from the Quietgiven if we are defeated. Some hold back their aid as leverage to advance their own politics. Some refuse because of old feuds. And some . . ." Stallworth's eyes showed dark concern. "Some, mostly in the north, have signed treaties with the Quiet, believing that we *cannot* win, and trying to broker for position once the fighting is over."

Layosah listened, horrified. Still, something had to be done. In a soft but urgent voice, she spoke again.

"Women do little more than breed more bodies to fill your suits of armor; men and boys bond over the thought of dying together; and widows and young girls are left to empty homes, porridge, and unsavory acts to earn a coin or else starve." She looked intently at him. "You must do better."

Silence followed her outburst. Neither the general nor Sheason seemed ready to speak. The silence was broken by the loud clap of boots approaching from behind.

"The rest are mounted, General. We are ready," said a young man in untarnished raiment.

"Then it is time," General Stallworth replied, his gaze still locked with Layosah's. "I go to join young Aelon," he said. A profound sadness and weariness deepened the lines in his face. "There is nothing more to be done, Anais. It is over."

He walked past her, and the rest of the men in the great war room followed. Shortly, she heard the thunder of countless hooves fade into the distance . Layosah regretted some of what she'd said. Not all. But some. The man, Stallworth, rode to his death—had planned to, even before she'd implored him to take action.

She was now alone with the Sheason, who watched her closely. After a time, he showed her a faint smile. Looking at him, she recalled tales of these renderers of the Will and their ability to restore life. She looked down at Audra.

Better to die in innocence and never know despair, she thought. *And if you save the lives of an entire people in doing so . . .*

She turned a hard stare on the Sheason. "I need to speak with you."

CB&O

THAT EVENING, LAYOSAH sat before the Sheason's hearth, which burned bright and warm with cedar logs. Audra slept cradled in her left arm, her face peaceful in the firelight. Layosah held in her free hand a small goblet of warmed wine, dusted with cinnamon. The soothing warmth of the fire and drink eased her after a long day in which memories of Aelon, her other boys, and her husband had threatened to haunt her.

But now, at rest in a deep leather-covered chair offered her by Sheason Nolaus in his neat and well-ordered house, the revenants began to return. She drank from her wine again, alone, as the Sheason had excused himself. With each passing moment, she became more certain that he'd left her by herself precisely so that she would be plagued by her dark thoughts.

She had seen in the renderer's eyes a keen and dangerous intelligence. Yet, he made her feel safe somehow. And even just being in his home gave her a bit of comfort.

Comfort enough that she opened herself up again to her memories, those revenants of the past, and recalled the day Eddock had returned from that first march . . . without Maalen.

He'd come into their home with two swords, and Layosah had known in her heart immediately what news he meant to share. No special messenger that first time. Instead, a father bearing his son's blade back to the boy's mother.

Eddock had stood before her, a broken man. "I tried to get to him, Layosah. He was too far . . ."

She'd said nothing, sure if she moved her knees would forsake her and drop her to the floor.

"We were separated in battle," Eddock said through tears he tried in vain to wipe away. "I fought back toward him. I fought . . ."

Layosah found some strength at last and moved to Eddock's side. Together they slumped to the floor of their small home. She wanted desperately to say something, but words failed her. She held his broad shoulders and felt him tremble.

"He was my son. I could not save him. I was a stone's throw away and they killed him as I rushed to help." Eddock lifted Maalen's sword up between them.

They knew the tradition of hanging the swords of the fallen on the walls of the family home. It was meant to serve as a reminder of the honor and sacrifice of the one who laid down his life for the good of his countrymen. But kneeling together on the floor of their home, where Maalen had taken his first steps, had run and laughed as children do, they could find little more in the sacrifice beyond their own grief. The child that had begun for them with a tease about milk had gone to his earth scarcely a man.

And Layosah had watched as her beloved tortured himself with blame for not having been able to save him.

In the years ahead, it would get no easier for either of them. The small lives that began with such joy ended prematurely, bringing sorrow and confusion and pain. Layosah could say of Eddock that at least his had ended in those same distant marches.

Now, with Aelon dead, they were all gone. All save Audra.

Layosah gazed upon her babe and forced herself to put the past away and feel content, if briefly, in being warm, with the taste of wine in her mouth, and thoughts of tomorrow distant enough not to be burdensome.

When her peace was nearly full, the Sheason returned, and sat with her near the fire. "What then, my dear woman, can I do for you?" He smiled as though he already knew the answer.

Layosah sipped her wine before answering. She had the feeling she would need to be careful with her words. "Your oath, Sheason. What is your oath?"

Nolaus folded his hands together in his lap. "What do you really wish to ask me, Anais Reyal? Are you asking if I am bound by my word to help you? If at any cost and in any circumstance my authority to command the Will must serve your need?" He did not smile as he said it, but neither was there rancor in his voice.

She stared back at him. That *was* what she wanted to know. But hearing it from the Sheason made her realize how selfish a question it was. Still, she nodded. She had to know.

Several moments passed. Finally, he nodded. "The answer is mostly yes. My calling is to use the gifts I bear to ease the suffering of those I can help." He paused, smiling again, but a touch more wanly. "But I cannot help all those who need help."

Layosah put down her goblet of wine and balled her fingers into a fist. "When a life hangs in the balance, will you *wish* to help? I need to know, Sheason. I need to know if there are limits to your favor."

A touch of severity lit the man's eyes. "Aye, Anais. There are." The stern look on the man's face remained for several moments; then, as though he was suddenly himself again, his wan smile returned. "Forgive me. My anger is not directed at you or even at your question. It is . . . that I must answer as I do."

Layosah gave him a questioning stare.

The Sheason looked back with appraising eyes. "You mean to do something unnatural, Anais. And you want my assurance that I can undo this thing, whatever it is. . . ."

She said nothing, her silence demanding an answer to her question.

"Very well," the man said. "I am bound, my good woman. That I can render the Will to aid and defend those who need my help is a gift I cherish. But it is not a power that should be used to arrogate godhood. And some things must not be done . . . or undone."

"You speak in riddles," she said sharply. "It is no wonder people are wary of your kind."

The man smiled, this time more fully, so that she could see his age in the wrinkles around his eyes. "People are wary of us, are they?" He chuckled softly. "Well, we shall have to endeavor to change such a perception."

"Then start now," she said, persistent. "You've said nothing that convinces me that there *are* limits to your favor. It sounds like a tradition steeped in myth. Arrogate godhood? Next you will tell me that the Charter itself binds you."

The Sheason's face drew taut with a grave expression. "Anais Reyal, these are not things to trifle with. What you speak of is part of the fabric of our world. You ask me what I will do when a life hangs in the balance, if I will *wish* to help. It is not as simple as you make it sound. I caution you. If there is a bloody deed in your heart, let it go. Don't seek from my gift . . . permission . . . to do harm."

And there it was. The Sheason had looked past her veiled questions to the heart of what she had come to ask. Layosah looked down at Audra, who slept soundly in her arms, and she began to cry. The losses of all those she loved seemed to pile upon her. She was alone now with this babe, and didn't believe she could support the weight of it all.

No. Something must be done.

Perhaps it would take a woman who had seen as many skies as she; and perhaps the despair in her heart would give rise to courage she could not otherwise summon.

In either case—and without the assurance she'd hoped to have from the Sheason—she had decided. She wondered if this was how it felt to walk upon the gallows without offering a struggle.

She stood and reached out her hand. The Sheason took it, and she wrapped her first finger around his thumb in token of both gratitude and apology. Nolaus cupped their clasped hands with his other palm and looked intently into her eyes.

"It does not mean I *cannot* help. It means I won't know until . . ."

Layosah found the strength to smile. "Put it out of your mind. You have helped me find my courage. That alone is help enough."

"Anais?"

"There is one thing more I would ask of you. The king. I should like to speak with him. You advise his general, so surely if I were with you he would listen to me. I know he walks the courtyard at dawn. Will you meet me there?"

The Sheason looked down at the child in her arms, a pained expression in his eyes. "It is what sets us apart, isn't it?" he said.

"What is that?"

But the Sheason did not reply, leaving the question for Layosah to answer. He only squeezed her hand and escorted her to the door. "I will meet you there," he said.

She tucked Audra close to her bosom and made her way home. *Tomorrow*, she thought, *tomorrow. . . .*

⋘⋙

HER ARMS FULL, Layosah walked slowly toward Solath Mahnus. The great seat of power—which housed the king, his council, and the court of judicature—rose up like a man-made mountain at the heart of Recityv. Parapets and spires stood high against a clear morning sky, lending to the place a grandeur that spoke of permanence and strength. She hoped her king possessed these same qualities.

When she arrived at the Wall of Remembrance, where the old stories had been carved in relief upon its surface, Sheason Nolaus awaited her. He nodded in greeting, and together they passed the gate guards, who nodded deferentially to the Sheason.

Beyond the wall, in the outer courtyard, the sun shone strong, lighting the wide stone stair at the east entrance. Dew on the steps glistened, steam rising as the sun warmed the stone.

King Baellor paced in the shadows to the left of the great stairs. Layosah shared a grave look with the Sheason and they moved toward their sovereign, their footfalls loud in the courtyard. As they approached, several men appeared as if from nowhere, preventing them from drawing too close. When the king looked up, he saw the Sheason and waved his men back.

The king's eyes were heavy with sleeplessness. "You do not often walk with me in the morning, Nolaus. To what do I owe the pleasure today?"

The Sheason raised a hand toward her. "I would ask that you give this woman a moment of your time, Your Majesty. I believe she has earned it."

183

King Baellor looked at Layosah. "I trust Nolaus's judgment. What would you speak with me about?"

She did not hesitate. "Yesterday I received the sword of my fifth son to die in your army's failed war." She raised the five swords of her five dead sons.

"Dear woman—"

"I don't seek your sympathy, my king," Layosah said quickly. She lowered the blades. "I seek your leadership. Your general tells me that efforts to find allies have failed in the past. It is troubling—"

"Indeed—"

"Troubling that you have failed to gain their support." Layosah spoke as if she were scolding one of her children.

The king looked at the Sheason. "Is this what you thought I should hear this morning, Nolaus? After yesterday?" Baellor then turned an intimidating stare on Layosah. "I regret the sacrifice you have made, Anais, but this is not the time to upbraid your king. Yesterday we sent every last man into the far country to meet those descending out of the Pall. I would remind you that many have made such sacrifices . . . are about to make such a sacrifice."

"That is precisely why I come this morning, my lord. Someone must speak for the blood of all those sent to die by foolish men. Someone with clear vision must show a king how to prevent more of his people from going early to their final earth." She spared a look at Audra, feelings of hope and despair vying in her heart when she considered the child's future.

"And your vision is clear?" The king's face was edged with impatience. "Dear woman, I do truly regret the loss of the sons you are asked to grieve for. It is no pleasure to me to send them to war."

His words were like a death sentence, leaving no room for argument, no room for compromise or collaboration. She had, then, the clearest thought she could remember ever having. Stallworth had said the war was bigger than Recityv. . . .

A great council. One to represent all the kingdoms of men.

"Then call them all at once," Layosah suggested, feeling some excitement at the simple notion.

Baellor's brow furrowed. "What? Who?"

"Send word to each of them, every king, every council, every nation, all at once. Let them know they are all being asked to come. That a seat awaits them. That it will be evident which seats remain vacant when you commence a great assembly of rulers to decide how to fight this war."

The king studied her face.

"Kings before you have sought allies and failed. And some nations, so it is said, secretly conspire with the enemy." Disgust filled her. "And some play politics while your people die. By the Skies, Your Majesty, if their conscience doesn't tell them the right choice, shame them into it!"

Her sovereign looked past her at the Sheason, a weary expression reclaiming his face. He appeared as though he might say something more, but instead he gently put a hand on Audra's head, offered a defeated smile, and started away toward an enclosed hallway that seemed to burrow into Solath Mahnus. Partway across the courtyard he stopped. She thought she heard him say, with his back still toward her, "It is not so simple." Then he moved on, his Emerit guard trailing him, until he vanished into Solath Mahnus.

When he had disappeared inside his sanctuary, Layosah frowned at the realization of what she must do next. Her heart ached as she walked slowly to the base of the broad stairs and looked up at the ceremonial entrance to this hall of kings.

She paused to kiss her last child. "I love you, little one," she said softly.

Then she mounted the first few steps to Solath Mahnus and, as violently as she could, she threw down upon the hard stone the five blades, five markers of the dead. The sixth blade—Eddock's own—she wore beneath her overcloak. The steel clattered loudly in the courtyard, drawing the attention of the handful of guards and some courtiers who were about their business early. In the broad court of stone also walked a few members of the Reconciliation clergy, deep in their robes and in their thoughts, softly talking into the morn.

All these, and a few whose purpose she could not determine, stopped and turned toward her. Just the attention she'd sought.

"It must end today!" she cried. "Please, hear me. I beg of you. We cannot suffer this war another year, another day, another hour."

The king's guards started toward her, their intention clear. The wall guards came, too, running from their post. Several courtiers stared, and the robed prelates began moving toward her.

They think I am mad or else that I am a zealot, and that I need their healing hands . . . perhaps, today, they are right. . . .

"Five children have I lost to this war! And my husband, besides. I am not the first to send my family to die. During centuries of ongoing battle, your women have been mere wombs, producing soldiers whose lives amount to nothing as they are slain by an enemy we cannot defeat; or daughters whose own wombs will be used to bear more of these ill-fated soldiers!"

The guards were close now, a few drawing their swords. Tears welled up as she thought of what she meant to do next. *Forgive me, Audra.* But in the depths of her anger and despair, she had decided, and she lifted her child high over her head.

"The war must stop! Or I will dash the child against the stone, and her blood will be upon your hands for not heeding my words!"

Everyone in the courtyard immediately stopped. Gasps rose in the silence, followed by a soft coo from her babe. She caught a look from the Sheason, his countenance drawn heavily with understanding.

"My lady," the closest guard said. "You needn't threaten the life of the child. We will hear what you have to say. Please, lower the infant."

Layosah laughed maniacally through her tears. "You think me a fool. Or mad. Or both. But we should all be so foolish and mad!"

Passersby from beyond the Wall of Remembrance began to come into the courtyard. Soon, a crowd had gathered, drawn by the spectacle of her grief. *Good.*

Still holding her baby high against the pale morning sky, she called, "This is my sixth child. All my sons went to war to defend us. All have perished. It has to stop!"

A low muttering of agreement rose from the crowd, even as more people streamed into the courtyard.

"My lady," the nearest guard said, "please. We needn't worry our fellow citizens unnecessarily. Come, let us go in. Perhaps we can speak with the king."

"I have spoken with the king," she said. "He is paralyzed by fear and outwitted by other sovereigns who better practice their statecraft."

The man-at-arms shook his head. "Be careful, my lady."

"No, sir," she replied softly, "Not anymore."

She looked out on the multitude, many of whom stared with rapt attention at Audra, who'd begun to fidget in Layosah's upraised hands.

"They tell us lies!" she shouted. "They assure us the war is in hand. But Stallworth has ridden toward his own death after telling me the war is bigger than his army, bigger than we can sustain or win. How many lives have been lost while our king refuses to do what is necessary?" She took a deep, shuddering breath. "We will not bear more children simply to see them marched into the far country to die! We are not your wombs of war! It must end!"

Soon, there remained no room in the courtyard. And she continued her ardent appeal, her demand! Each time she railed anew, the great crowd roared its approval. Layosah had seen mobs before, but this was not the same. She saw in no man's or woman's eyes irrational intention. They were tired and scared. But for that moment, in the strong light of an eastern sun, the pall of death and despair lifted, caused by their collective desire to see an end to a war that was generations old.

Even as she held the king's guard at bay with the threat of killing her only living child.

Have I gone too far? But I cannot stop. Audra, forgive me, I cannot stop.

She stared out at the great crowd, silent for a very long time. A hush fell over the courtyard. Softly, she spoke. "I would rather take my daughter's life here, today . . . myself . . . than watch her grow up to bear children of her own that will only die or perpetuate this endless cycle of death." She surveyed as many of the onlookers as she could. "These warmongers should have the resolve of a mother who is willing to send her children against the Quiet . . . who is willing to *kill* her own child to deny them one more womb of war."

And on she spoke. All that day.

When her arms tired, she lowered Audra and held her close, but then drew Eddock's sword and held it firmly, ready if it should come to that. And as she stood with Audra in one hand, and her beloved's weapon in the other, she continued to rail against her king and her general and her nation for failing generations of families.

For three days she remained on the east steps of Solath Mahnus, decrying all those whom she could think of now only as murderers. When she had to, she fed her babe, keeping a watchful eye on the Emerit guards stationed nearby, one hand still holding tight her sword.

The first night, she sat upon the cool stone to rest and kept a dark silent vigil with the great crowd. But she did not leave. Would not. There was no going back to the life she had lived. One way or another, something would change here at the steps of Solath Mahnus.

When the second day broke in the eastern sky, she stood again and started to speak. At times, she recounted memories of her dead children. From the steps, she could see the crowd stretched beyond the courtyard, beyond the Wall of Remembrance. The great concourse beyond the wall, and the nearby streets, stood packed with more citizens yet, and she could hear men calling back to those too far to hear her, relaying her words. She began to grow weary, but the fire of her own anger and the shouts of agreement gave her strength to continue.

When the second night came, torches were lit, and she imagined that these citizens would return to their homes. They did not. Instead, they again sat, as they had the night before, and together kept a silence. It seemed as if they felt that they must watch with her, that what was happening held import for them all, and so they would not retire to their homes.

When Layosah stood on the morning of her third day at the steps of Solath Mahnus, she wondered if she would, after all, be able to force those who pontificated in vaulted rooms to listen and understand and act . . . if she still had the courage to go through with what she'd planned if she could not compel them by words alone. Yes, the blood she promised to spill would be upon their heads, but only if she had enough will to see it through. After two days of calling on her king to hear her, she began to fear she could do neither.

And if she failed, she felt, the deaths of her five sons, and of her beloved, would have been in vain. More than this, her daughter would inherit Layosah's fate. Yet for all that, as her third day wore on, speaking to the people and demanding that her sovereign take action, she lost much of her zeal, despair gripping her.

As dusk settled over the courtyard on the third day, Layosah's strength was nearly gone. Weary to the bone, she could barely stand. She began to fade, and her eyes threatened to close despite all her efforts. Just as the torches were lit, she caught a glimpse of movement, and forced herself up straight in time to stop the king's men in their rush to seize her.

With a surge of anger flooding through her, she gathered her strength and held Audra high, believing that it would be the last time she could do so. Suddenly she felt as if she had lost herself. *Who am I? How can I do this?* Audra was crying—a sound she heard as though it came from far away. She felt tortured, wounded . . . mad. And in the next moment, fury overcame her, righteous anger that gave her strength in her conviction and clarity of purpose.

She glared at the king's guard, then looked out once more over those keeping vigil with her. The citizens got to their feet as she prepared to speak, her voice now a hoarse rasp.

"My grandmother raised soldiers. My mother, too. And now I . . . I stand here on these chiseled steps with a child. My family's blood is good enough to be spilled for Recityv to protect her from the Quiet, but her king will not do what is needful so that my daughter will not likewise know the pain of war tidings."

Layosah began to tremble and teeter. Her strength, even fueled by her anger, was flagging.

"I lift my child here and call upon King Seachen Baellor one last time to form a council to represent *all* the people. He must look beyond his borders, mend broken alliances, call for truces to old feuds. Shame any who deny! All must come. All must be convinced to stand with us!"

Her arms were failing fast. She locked her elbows to keep Audra held aloft. Sweat beaded on her face, running down her cheeks and neck. She felt like she was living one of the many nightmares she had so often lately. Her vision blurred, so that she saw only streaks of firelight from the many torches that blazed in the night.

The multitude clamored for something to be done. Part of her believed they wished to watch her see it through, make good on her threat—bloodlust in their cries. But in some moments, she heard more truly, as the war-weary people of Recityv began to chant for the king to answer Layosah's demand.

In the extremity of her need, she called out one last time: "Or else I should rather dash my babe on this stone stair and snuff her life, than see her bear another generation to war!"

The greatest tumult yet rose from those gathered in the courtyard and in the streets around Solath Mahnus.

As the din died down, one of the guards crept close enough that she heard him when he said, "The king does not yield to threats or demands. You will have to kill you child or stand down."

Layosah turned to the Sheason, who had been close by throughout her stand here, and whose face still was a mask of doleful understanding. He returned her stare and slowly shook his head. He would not help her if she did this thing.

I must not yield. So much depends on it. . . .

She knew that once she threw down her child, her life was forfeit. Not by dint of law. But because her mind and soul would be broken. The only reassuring thought was that of walking slowly into a still, cold lake until her feet could no longer touch the bottom and she could slip soundlessly to her own death.

She wept openly, helplessly ranting against her own plan to kill Audra, even as she prepared to cast the child down on the steps of her king's castle. The throng wailed, loud in her ears. The guards watched, their eyes wide.

She began to rock back on her heels to give her arms momentum. She closed her eyes, because she couldn't bear to watch her darling Audra fly to her death, but in the instant of her blindness, she saw the faces of her family. Most of all, she saw Eddock and the moments they had shared in joy and pain over the lives they'd created, the family they'd shared.

With those images in her mind and the sound of the great crowd in her ears, she heard through the din the sharp cry of a child. It wasn't Audra. The sound struck her, and she opened her eyes, casting her gaze out over the thousands gathered in the courtyard and beyond the Wall of Remembrance. She suddenly took note of fathers holding up sons so that they could see, young girls seated near their parents' feet, mothers holding infants of their own.

So many young lives, newly begun, and brought into the world by parents . . . who still . . .

Layosah shot a look at Sheason Nolaus and found a warm smile. She had found the answer to the question she'd posed him a few nights earlier. She understood now that she could not have fully appreciated simply being given that answer. She had to feel it for herself:

It's what sets us apart, isn't it?

What's that?

Hope.

The realization did not come as a new or profound revelation, but rather as a simple, quiet truth. She, like so many others, lived on. They loved, and had families in the face of uncertainty . . . and hoped.

Her vision blurred from weariness. Her strength began to fail. She looked up at the daughter she still held aloft, preparatory to an act of desperation and hopelessness.

Layosah let out a heartrending cry: "No!"

She collapsed upon the steps, folding Audra into her chest, safe and crying. She huddled over her, feeling broken and bitter and shamed. But for all the dark moments and feelings, she could not let the last good thing she and Eddock had done together be destroyed, certainly not by her own hand. Her love of her husband and of her little one simply would not allow it.

Silence followed. Only the hum of torches, as her child quieted against her breast.

She did not know how long she had lain there when a hand firmly gripped her shoulder. *The guards*, she thought, who would now strip her child from her and lock her in the depths of Solath Mahnus. But when she looked up, she saw the thoughtful face of her king. He looked ready to say something, his eyes alight in the flames of nearby torches. But he remained silent, staring at her and her child. Perhaps it was her fatigue, or the ache in her spirit after so much loss, or the numbing fear of what would now happen to her, but whatever the reason, Layosah thought she saw change in her king. She stared up into his dark, wondering eyes.

The man then again put a hand gently on Audra's head, and stood to face the great multitude. He met their expectant stares, and she thought he might make some grand speech to allay their worries, perhaps even commend her willingness to do her child harm to rouse him from the depths of his keep. He did neither.

After several long moments, and still looking out over the people who'd gathered to support Layosah's defense of another generation of children—trying to save them from the horrors of war—he spoke instead to a captain of his personal guard, one she'd not noticed before.

"Call the birders, bring heralds to me here, now." He said nothing more before he fell silent again and waited.

Shortly, those summoned made their way through the crowd, gathering around the king. He took up a quill and ink and wrote out a message on a parchment. While the crowd watched, his men copied the short script several dozen times on individual sheets.

When the task was done, the king nodded to his captain. "Make way," the captain said, gesturing for the people to part, as horses were brought to the steps of Solath Mahnus.

The heralds mounted. The birders fastened notes to the legs of small raptors. When stillness reclaimed the outer courtyard, King Baellor spoke with a resoluteness Layosah could not remember ever hearing.

"Recityv will stand alone no longer. If your sons and daughters are called upon to perish for her sake, it will be at the side of children raised in kingdoms other than our own." He stopped, seeming to consider what next to say. "No, not to perish. To vanquish. To end our centuries of suffering. I've been a fool, quailing before the politics of alliance like a coward, beneath the politics that make alliances so fraught with difficulty. I will be a fool no more."

He then raised a hand. At that signal, the birds took flight, and the mounted heralds stormed from the courtyard in a thundering of hooves over stone. Layosah watched with weary eyes, the air fairly filled with birds winging skyward into the darkness, carrying the king's message, and horses gaining speed as they passed the Wall of Remembrance, their riders bent low in the saddle, racing with their majesty's words tucked into their shirts.

It was done. She had made him see. At some cost that she felt she would later understand—the awful notion of what she'd almost done here—she'd made him see.

Over the flutter of wings and clatter of hooves, the great crowd broke into a deafening chorus of cheers. The king did not stand to receive any of it, but instead turned and bent near to her.

"You've reminded me of my oath, Anais. Thank you. This convocation of seated kings and other rulers . . . I will endeavor to be as compelling with them as you have been with me." He reached down and helped her to her feet. The king then gathered the swords strewn nearby, and, carrying them himself beneath one arm, he assisted her up the steps toward Solath Mahnus. "You will rest. Then you will tell me of the men who carried these swords. Each one. Sparing nothing."

Together they ascended the stone stairs as the relieved and hopeful cries of the city faded behind them.

Read on for a preview of the

AUTHOR'S DEFINITIVE EDITION OF

THE UNREMEMBERED

by

PETER ORULLIAN

AVAILABLE APRIL 2015

THE
UNREMEMBERED

The Vault of Heaven

"One is forced to conclude that while the gods had the genius to create music, they didn't understand its power. There's a special providence in that, lads. It also ought to scare the last hell out of you."

> —Taken from the rebuttal made by the philosopher
> Lour Nail in the College of Philosophy
> during the Succession of Arguments on Continuity

WHAT HADN'T BEEN BURNED, had been broken. Wood, stone . . . flesh. Palamon stood atop a small rise, surveying the wound that was a city. Beside him, Dossolum kept a god's silence. Black smoke rose in straight pillars, its slow ascent unhindered by wind. None had been left alive. None. This wasn't blind, angry retaliation. This was annihilation. This was breakage of a deeper kind than wood or stone or flesh. This was breakage of the spirit.

Ours . . . and theirs, Palamon thought. He shook his head with regret. "The Veil isn't holding those you sent into the Bourne."

Dossolum looked away to the north. "This place is too far gone. Is it any wonder we're leaving it behind?"

"You're the Voice of the Council," Palamon argued. "If you stay, the others will stay. Then together—"

"The decision has been made," Dossolum reminded him. "Some things cannot be redeemed. Some things shouldn't."

Palamon clenched his teeth against further argument. He still had entreaties to make. Better not to anger the only one who could grant his requests. But it was hard. He'd served those who lay dead in the streets below him, just as he'd served the Creation Council. *Someone* should speak for the dead.

"You don't have to stay," Dossolum offered again. "None of the Sheason need stay. There's little you can do here. What we began will run its course. You might slow it"—he looked back at the ruined city—"but eventually, it will all come to this."

Palamon shook his head again, this time in defiance. "You don't know that."

Dossolum showed him a patient look. "We don't go idly. The energy required to right this . . . Better to start fresh, with new matter. In another place." He looked up at evening stars showing in the east.

"Most of the Sheason are coming with you," Palamon admitted.

"All but you, I think." Dossolum dropped his gaze back to the city. "It's not going to be easy here. Even with the ability to render the Will . . ."

Palamon stared at burned stone and tracts of land blackened to nothing. "Because some of those who cross the Veil have the same authority," he observed.

"Not only that." Dossolum left it there.

"Then strengthen the Veil," Palamon pled. "Make it the protection you meant it to be." He put a hand on Dossolum's arm. "Please."

In the silence that followed, a soft sound touched the air. A song. A lament. Palamon shared a look with Dossolum, then followed the sound. They descended the low hill. And step by step the song grew louder, until they rounded a field home. Beside a shed near a blackened pasture sat a woman with her husband's head in her lap. She stroked his hair as she sang. Not loud. Not frantic. But anguished, like a deep, slow saddening moved through her.

Tears had cleaned tracks down her field-dirty cheeks. Or maybe it was char. Like the smell of burning all around them.

But she was alive. Palamon had thought everyone here dead.

She looked up at them, unsurprised. Her vacant stare might not have seen them at all. She kept singing.

Palamon noticed toys now beside the home.

"The city wasn't enough," Palamon said, anger welling inside him. "They came into the fields to get them all."

The woman sang on. Her somber melody floated like cottonwood seed, brushing past them soft and earthward.

Dossolum stood and listened a long while. He made no move to comfort the woman, or to revive the man. His face showed quiet appreciation. Only when she'd begun to repeat her song did he finally speak. And then in a low tone, like a counterpoint.

"Very well, Palamon." Dossolum continued to watch the woman grieve. "Write it all down. Everything we tried to do. Our failure. The Bourne and those we sent there. The war to do so." He grew quiet. "A story of desolation."

Tentatively, Palamon asked, "And do what with it?"

The woman's song turned low and throaty and bare.

Dossolum gave a sad smile. "To some we'll give a gift of song. They'll sing the story you write. And so long as they do, the Veil will be added to. Strengthened."

He nodded, seeming satisfied. "But it will be a suffering to sing it. Leaving them *diminished*."

"Thank you, Dossolum." Palamon then silently thanked the woman who mourned in front of them. Her mortal sorrow had touched his friend's eternal heart.

"Don't thank me." Dossolum's eyes showed their first hint of regret. "Like every good intention, a song can fade."

Palamon looked up at the same evening stars Dossolum had watched a moment ago. "Or it might be sung even after the light of the stars has fled the heavens."

"I hope you're right, my friend. I hope you're right."

BOOK ONE

THE UNREMEMBERED

STILLBORN

*"The Church of Reconciliation—Reconciliationists, so called—
preach that the Framers left behind protections. And these
protections were given proper names. Names we've forgotten.
Would these protections cease, then, to serve? Or would we
have to question the origins of the doctrine?"*
—Excerpt from *Rational Suppositions*,
a street tract disseminated by the League of Civility

AN OPEN DOOR . . .

Tahn Junell drew his bow, and kicked his mount into a
dead run. They descended the shallow dale in a rush toward that
open door. Toward home.

The road was muddy. Hooves threw sludge. Lightning arced in
the sky. A peal of thunder shattered the silence and pushed through
the small vale in waves. It echoed outward through the woods in
diminishing tolls.

The whispering sound of rain on trees floated toward him. The
soft smells of earth and pollen hung on the air, charged with the

coming of another storm. Cold perspiration beaded on his forehead and neck.

An open door . . .

His sister, Wendra, wouldn't leave the door open to the chill.

Passing the stable, another bolt of white fire erupted from the sky, this time striking the ground. It hit at the near end of the vale. Thunder exploded around him. A moment later, a scream rose from inside his home. His mount reared, tugging at his reins and throwing Tahn to the ground before racing for the safety of the stable. Tahn lost his bow and began frantically searching the mud for the dropped weapon. The sizzle of falling rain rose, a lulling counterpoint to the screams that continued from inside. Something crashed to the floor of the cabin. Then a wail rose up. It sounded at once deep in the throat, like the thunder, and high in the nose like a child's mirth.

Tahn's heart drummed in his ears and neck and chest. His throat throbbed with it. Wendra was in there! He found his bow. Shaking the mud and water from the bowstring and quickly cleaning the arrow's fletching on his coat, he sprinted for the door. He nocked the arrow and leapt to the stoop.

The home had grown suddenly still and quiet.

He burst in, holding his aim high and loose.

An undisturbed fire burned in the hearth, but everything else in his home lay strewn or broken. The table had been toppled on its side, earthen plates broken into shards across the floor. Food was splattered against one wall and puddled near a cooking pot in the far corner. Wendra's few books sat partially burned near the fire, their thrower's aim not quite sure.

Tahn saw it all in a glance as he swung his bow to the left where Wendra had tucked her bed up under the loft.

She lay atop her quilts, knees up and legs spread.

Absent gods, no!

Then, within the shadows beneath the loft, Tahn saw it, a hulking mass standing at the foot of Wendra's bed. It hunched over, too tall to remain upright in the nook beneath the upper room. Its hands cradled something in a blanket of horsehair. The smell of sweat and blood and new birth commingled with the aroma of the cooking pot.

The figure slowly turned its massive head toward him. Wendra looked too, her eyes weary but alive with fright. She weakly reached one arm toward him, mouthing something, but unable to speak.

In a low, guttural voice the creature spoke, "*Quillescent* all around." It rasped words in thick, glottal tones.

Then it stepped from beneath the loft, its girth massive. The fire lit the creature's fibrous skin, which moved independent of the muscle and bone beneath. Ridges and rills marked its hide, which looked like elm bark. But pliable. It uncoiled its left arm from the blanket it held to its chest, letting its hand hang nearly to its knees. From a leather sheath strapped to its leg, the figure drew a long knife. Around the hilt it curled its hand—three talonlike fingers with a thumb on each side, its palm as large as Tahn's face. Then it pointed the blade at him.

Tahn's legs began to quiver. Revulsion and fear pounded in his chest. This was a nightmare come to life. This was Bar'dyn, a race out of the Bourne. One of those given to Quietus, the dissenting god.

"We go," the Quietgiven said evenly. It spoke deep in its throat. Its speech belied a sharp intelligence in its eyes. When it spoke, only its lips moved. The skin on its face remained thick and still, draped loosely over protruding cheekbones that jutted like shelves beneath its eyes. Tahn glimpsed a mouthful of sharp teeth.

"Tahn," Wendra managed, her voice hoarse and afraid.

Blood spots marked her white bed-dress, and her body seemed frozen in a position that prevented her from straightening her legs. Tahn's heart stopped.

Against its barklike skin, the Bar'dyn held cradled in a tightly woven blanket of mane and tail . . . Wendra's child.

Pressure mounted in Tahn's belly: hate, helplessness, confusion, fear. All a madness like panicked wings in his mind. He was supposed to protect her, keep her safe, especially while she carried this child. A child come of rape. But a child she looked forward to. Loved.

Worry and anger rushed inside him. "No!"

His scream filled the small cabin, leaving a deeper silence in its wake. But the babe made no sound. The Bar'dyn only stared. On the stoop and roof, the patter of rain resumed, like the sound of a distant waterfall. Beyond it, Tahn heard the gallop of hooves on the muddy road. *More Bar'dyn? His friends?*

He couldn't wait for either. In a shaky motion, he drew his aim on the creature's head. The Bar'dyn didn't move. There wasn't even defiance in its expression.

"I'll take you *and* the child. Velle will be pleased." It nodded at its own words, then raised its blade between them.

Velle? Dead gods, they've brought a renderer of the Will with them!

Tahn's aim floundered from side to side. Weariness. Cold fear.

The Bar'dyn stepped toward him. Tahn's mind raced, and fastened upon one thought. *The hammer.* He focused on that mark on the back of his bow hand, visually tracing its lines and feeling it with his mind. A simple, solid thing. He didn't remember where he'd gotten the scar or brand, but it seemed intentional. And it grounded him. With that moment of reassurance, his hands steadied, and he drew deeper into the pull, bringing his aim on the Bar'dyn's throat.

"Put the child down." His voice trembled even as his mouth grew dry.

The Bar'dyn paused, looking down at the bundle it carried. The creature then lifted the babe up, causing the blanket to slip to the floor. Its massive hand curled around the little one's torso. The infant still glistened from its passage out of Wendra's body, its skin red and purple in the sallow light of the fire.

"Child came dead, grub."

Sadness and anger welled again in Tahn. His chest heaved at the thought of Wendra giving birth in the company of this vile thing, having her baby taken at the moment of life into its hands. *Was the child dead at birth, or had the Bar'dyn killed it?* Tahn glanced again at Wendra. She was pale. Sadness etched her features. He watched her close her eyes against the Bar'dyn's words.

The rain now pounded the roof. But the sound of heavy footfalls on the road was clear, close, and Tahn abandoned hope of escape. One Bar'dyn, let alone several, might tear him apart, but he intended to send this one to the abyss, for Wendra, for her dead child.

He prepared to fire his bow, allowing time enough to speak the old, familiar words: "I draw with the strength of my arms, but release as the Will allows."

But he couldn't shoot.

He struggled to disobey the feeling, but it stretched back into that part of his life he couldn't remember. He had always spoken the words, always. He didn't release of his own choice. He always followed the quiet intimations that came after he spoke those words.

Tahn relaxed his aim and the Bar'dyn nodded approval. "Bound to Will," it said. The words rang like the cracking of timber in the confines of the small home. "But first to watch this one go." The Bar'dyn turned toward Wendra.

"No!" Tahn screamed again, filling the cabin with denial. Denial of the Bar'dyn.

Denial of his own impotence.

The sound of others came up the steps. Tahn was surrounded. They would all die!

He spared a last look at his sister. "I'm sorry," he tried to say, but it came out in a husk.

Her expression of confusion and hurt and disappointment sank deep inside him.

If he couldn't kill the creature, he could at least try to prevent it from hurting her.

Before he could move, his friends shot through the door. They got between Tahn and the Bar'dyn. They fought the creature. They filled his home with a clash of wills and swordplay and shouted oaths. Chaos churned around him. And all he could do was watch Wendra curl deeper into her bed. Afraid. Heartsick.

The creature out of the Bourne finally turned and crashed through the cabin's rear wall, rushing into the dark and the storm with Wendra's dead child. They did not give chase.

Tahn turned from the hole in the wall and went to Wendra's side. Blood soaked the coverlet, and cuts in her wrists and hands told of failed attempts to ward off the Bar'dyn. Her cheeks sagged; she looked pale and spent. She lay crying silent tears.

He'd stood twenty feet away with a clear shot at the Bar'dyn and had done nothing. The lives of his sister and her child had hung in the balance, and he'd done nothing. The old words had told him the draw was wrong. He'd followed that feeling over the defense of his sister. Why?

It was an old ache and frustration, believing himself bound to the impressions those words stirred inside him. But never so much as now.

CHAPTER ONE

OLD WORDS

"It is the natural condition of man to strive for certainty. It is also his condition not to find it. Not for long, anyway. Even a star may wander."

—From *Commentary on Categoricals*,
a reader for children nominated to
Dimnian cognitive training

TRANQUIL DARKNESS STRETCHED to the horizon. Small hours. Moments of quiet, of peace. Moments when faraway stars seemed as close and familiar as friends. Moments of night before the east would hint of sunrise. Tahn stepped into these small hours. Into the chill night air. He went to spend time with the stars. To imagine dawn. As he always had.

There was a kind of song in it all. A predictable rhythm and melody that might only be heard by one willing to remain quiet and unmoving long enough to note the movement of a star. It could be heard in the phases of the moons. It was by turns a single deep sonorous note, large as a russet sun setting slow, and then a great chorus, as when showers of shooting stars brightened the night sky.

They were harmonies across ages, heard during the brief measure of a life. But only if one paused, as Tahn did, to watch and listen.

He stood at the edge of the High Plains of Sedagin. The bluff rose a thousand strides off the flatlands below. Stars winked like sparkling bits of glass on a dark tablecloth. His breath clouded the night, and droplets hung like frozen tears from low scrub and sage.

He looked east and let his thoughts come naturally. Deep into the far reaches of the sky he let them wander, his emotions and hopes struggling for form with the stars. He traced the constellations, some from old stories, some from memories whose sources were lost to him. A half-full moon had risen high, its surface bright and clear. The pale outline of the darkened portion appeared a ghostly halo.

Tahn closed his eyes and let his thoughts run out even further, imagining the sun; imagining its warmth and radiance, its calm, sure track across the heavens. He imagined the sky changing color in the east from black to violet to sea blue and finally the color of clear, shallow water. He pictured more color as sunlight came to the forest and touched its leaves and cones and limbs. He envisioned those first moments of dawn, the unfurling of flower petals to its light, its glint on rippling water, steam rising from warming loam. And as he always did at such a moment, Tahn felt like part of the land, another leaf to be touched by the sun. His thoughts coalesced into the singular moment of sunrise and another hope risen up from the night, born again with quiet strength.

He opened his eyes to the dark skies and the foliate pattern of stars. In the east, the first intimation of day arose as the black hinted of violet hues. A quiet relief filled him, and he took a lungful of air.

Another day would come. And pass. Until the beautiful, distant stars returned, and he came again to watch. Until someday, when either he or the sun would not rise. And the song would end.

He lingered, enjoying a moment's peace. They'd been on the road more days than he could remember. Chased by the Quiet. Chased since the night he'd let Wendra down, failed to shoot when she'd needed him, when the Quiet took her child. Tahn shook his head with guilt at the memory of it.

And now here he was. Weeks later. Far from home. Just tonight they'd climbed this plateau, arriving after midnight. After dark hour.

He took a long breath, relaxing in the stillness.

The sound of boots over frost-covered earth startled him. He turned to see Vendanj come to join him.

Even the shadows of night couldn't soften the hard edges of the man. Vendanj wore determination the way another does his boots. Carried it in his eyes and shoulders. Vendanj was a member of the Sheason Order, those who rendered the Will—that melding of spirit and body, energy and matter. The Sheason weren't well known in the Hollows, Tahn's home. And Tahn was learning that beyond the Hollows, the Sheason weren't always welcome. Were even distrusted.

Vendanj came up beside him, and stared out over the plains far and away below. He didn't rush to clutter the silence with words. And they watched together for a time.

After long moments, Vendanj eyed Tahn with wry suspicion. "You do this every morning." It wasn't a question.

Tahn returned the wry grin. "How would you know? You follow me everywhere?"

"Just until we reach the Saeculorum," Vendanj answered.

They shared quiet laughter over that. It was a rare jest from Vendanj. But it was a square jest, the kind with truth inside. Because they were, in fact, going to the Saeculorum—mountains at the far end of the Eastlands. Several months' travel from here.

"For as long as I can remember," Tahn finally admitted, "I've gotten up early to watch the sunrise. Habit now, I guess."

Vendanj folded his arms as he stared east. "It's more than a habit, I suspect."

And he was right. It was more like a compulsion. A need. To stand with the stars. Imagine daybreak.

But Vendanj didn't press, and fell silent again for a time.

Into the silence, distantly, came again the sound of footfalls over hard dirt. The chill air grew . . . tight. Dense. It seemed to press on Tahn. Panic tightened his gut. Vendanj held up a hand for Tahn not to speak. A few moments later, up the trail of the cliff face came a figure, unhurried. Directly toward them.

Soon, the moon brought the shape into focus. A man. He wore an unremarkable coat, buttoned high against the chill. No cowl or robe or weapon. No smile of greeting. No frown. It was the man's utter lack of expression that frightened Tahn most, as if feeling had gone out of him.

Twenty strides from them, the other stopped, returning the bluff to silence. The figure stared at them through the dark. Stared at them with disregard.

Softer than a whisper, "Velle," Vendanj said.

My dying gods.

Velle were Quiet renderers of the Will. Like Sheason, but followers of the dissenting god.

The silence stretched between them, dawn still a long while away.

Into the stillness, the other spoke, his voice soft and low. "Your legs will tire, Sheason. And we will be there when they do." He pointed at Tahn. "Send me the boy, and let's be done."

"It would do you no good," Vendanj replied. "If not the boy, there are others."

The Velle nodded. "We know. And this one isn't the first you've driven like a mule." The man's eyes shifted to Tahn. "What has he told you, Quillescent?"

Tahn didn't really understand the question, and didn't reply. He only took his bow down from his shoulder.

The Velle shook his head slowly in disappointment. "You don't have the energy to fight me, Sheason. You've spent too much already."

"I appreciate your concern," Vendanj said, another surprising jest from the usually severe man.

The Velle hadn't taken its eyes from Tahn. "And what about you, with your little bow? Are you going to ask your gods if I should die, and shoot me down?" The expression in the man's face changed, but only by degrees. *More* indifferent. Careworn to the bone, beyond feeling.

He knows. He knows the words I speak when I draw.

The Velle dropped its chin. "Ask it." The words were an invitation, a challenge. And the chill air bristled when the Velle spoke them. Grasses and low sage bent away from the man as though they would flee.

Vendanj held up a hand. "You've strolled onto the Sedagin plain, my Quiet friend. A thousand swords and more. Go back the way you came."

A slow smile touched the Velle's face. A wan smile lacking warmth or humor. And even that looked unnatural, as though he were unaccustomed to smiling at all. "I don't take care for myself, Sheason. That is a *man's* weakness. And there'll be no heroes this time." He raised a hand, and Vendanj let out an explosive exhale, as if his chest were suddenly being pressed by boulders.

In a single motion, Tahn raised his bow and drew an arrow. *I draw with the strength of my arms, but release as the Will allows.*

The quiet confirmation came. The Velle should die.

Tahn caught a glimpse of a more genuine smile on the Quiet's lips before he let his arrow fly. An unconcerned flip of the Velle's wrist, and the arrow careened high and harmless out over the bluff's edge.

Vendanj dropped to his knees, struggling against some unseen force. Tahn had to disrupt the Velle's hold on the Sheason somehow. But before he could move, a deep shiver started in his chest as though his body were a low cello string being slowly played. And with the resonance rushed the memory of his failure to shoot the Bar'dyn that had come into his and Wendra's home, taken her child.

Except it seemed more raw now. Like alcohol poured on a fresh cut.

And that wasn't all. Other memories stirred. Lies he'd told. Insults he'd offered. Though he couldn't recall them with exactness. They were half formed, but sharpening.

He was maybe seven. A fight. Friends. Some kind of contest to settle . . .

Tahn began to tremble violently. His teeth ached and felt ready to shatter. His mind burned hot with regret and self-loathing. He dropped face-first beside Vendanj, and curled into a ball against the pain.

Vendanj still wasn't breathing, but managed to thrust an open palm at the Velle. The Quiet man grimaced, and Vendanj drew a harsh-sounding breath, his face slick with sweat in the moonlight.

Tahn's own inner ache subsided, and the quaking in his body stopped. Briefly. The Velle dropped to both knees and drove its hands into the hard soil. Blackness flared, and the Quiet man looked suddenly refreshed. This time, it simply stared at Vendanj. The earth between them whipped, low sage tearing away. But Vendanj was prepared, and kept his feet and breath when some force hit him, exploding in a fury of spent energy. The Sheason's lean face had drawn into a grim expression, and he began shaking his head.

The Velle glanced at Tahn and tremors wracked his body again. With them came his insecurities about childhood years lost to memory. As if they didn't matter. As if *he* didn't matter, except to raise his bow and repeat those godsforsaken words, *I draw with the strength* . . .

As the Velle caressed him with this deep resonant pain, a shadow flashed behind the other. Light and quick.

A moment later the Velle's back arched, his eyes wide in surprise. Tahn's tremors stopped. Vendanj lowered his arms. The Velle fell forward, and standing there was Mira Far, of the Far people. Her pale skin awash in moonlight. Only a Far could have gotten behind a Velle without being noticed. Looking at her, Tahn felt a different kind of tug inside. One that was altogether more appealing.

For the third time that morning, boots over hard earth interrupted the dark morning stillness. A hundred strides behind Mira three Bar'dyn emerged on the trail. At first they only walked. Then, seeing the downed Velle, they broke into a run, a kind of reasoned indifference in their faces. Their massive frames moved with grace, and power, as their feet pounded against the cold earth.

Tahn reached for an arrow. Mira dropped into one of her Latae stances, both swords raised. Vendanj gasped several breaths, still trying to steady himself from his contest with the Velle. "Take the Bar'dyn down," he said, his voice full of hateful prejudice.

Tahn pulled three successive draws, thinking the old words in an instant and firing at the closest Bar'dyn. The first arrow bounded harmlessly off the creature's barklike skin. But the next two struck it in the neck. It fell with a heavy crunch on the frost-covered soil.

The remaining two descended on Mira first. She ducked under a savage swipe of a long rounded blade and came up with a thrust into the creature's groin. Not simply an attack on its tender parts, but a precise cut into the artery that ran alongside them—something she'd taught him during one of their many conversations.

The Bar'dyn shrugged off the blow and rushed onward toward Tahn. In a few moments it would grow sluggish from blood loss, and finally fall. Tahn had only to keep a distance.

The other Quiet pushed ahead faster, closing on Tahn. Mira took chase, but even with her gift of speed wouldn't reach it before it got to him. Tahn pulled a deep draw. The Bar'dyn raised a forearm to protect its neck, and barreled closer.

"Take it down!" Vendanj began raising a hand, clearly weakened. The Sheason had rendered the Will so often lately. And he'd had little time to recover.

Tahn breathed out, steadied his aim, spoke the words in his mind, and let fly. The arrow hit true, taking the Bar'dyn's left eye.

No cry or scream. It stutter-stepped, and kept on. Its expression was as impassive as before—not fury, reason.

Tahn drew again. This arrow struck the Quiet's knee, as he'd intended. But it shattered against the armor-hard skin there. It was almost too close to fire again, but Tahn pulled a quick draw, Mira a half step behind the creature, and fired at its mouth. The arrow smashed through its teeth and went out through its cheek. The Bar'dyn's face stretched in a mask of pain. Then it leveled its eyes again and leapt at Tahn.

It was too late to avoid the Quiet. Tahn braced himself. The massive creature drove him to the ground under its immense weight. Tahn lost his breath, couldn't cry out. He could feel blood on his face. The Bar'dyn shifted to take hold of him.

It propped itself up with one arm, and stared down at Tahn with its indifferent eyes. "You don't understand," it said with a thick, glottal voice.

The Bar'dyn began to roll, pulling Tahn with it, as if it might try to carry him away. A moment later, it stopped moving. Mira. She pulled her blade from the creature's head. Then she turned on the wounded Bar'dyn, who was now staggering toward them, weak from loss of blood.

The last Quiet fell. It panted for several moments, then went still.

CHAPTER TWO

KEEPING PROMISES

"And a Sheason known as Portis came into the court of King Yusefi, king of Kuren, and demanded he keep his pledge to the Second Promise and send men to help the Sedagin in the far North. But Yusefi denied him. Whereupon Portis rendered the king's blood boiling hot and burned him alive inside. To my knowledge, this is the first recorded instance of Sheason violence against man."

> —An account of the Castigation, from the pages of the Kuren Court diarist

WARM BAR'DYN BLOOD STEAMED in the moonlight. Tahn scrambled away from the dead Quiet and sat heavily on the cold ground. His heart hammered in his chest. There was no getting used to this.

And now a Velle! What had it done to him? He still felt it. Like vibrations of thought or emotion. Deep down.

"All the way to the Saeculorum," Tahn said, repeating the joke Vendanj had made before this latest Quiet attack. Now it just sounded exhausting. Impossible.

Vendanj eased himself down to sit near Tahn. "It's good you're handy with a bow."

Mira crouched in front of them, keeping her feet under her—always ready. "Velle. That's new." She was looking at Vendanj.

He nodded. "But not surprising. And not the last we'll see of them."

"There's a happy thought," Tahn said without humor. "Seems like every damn day another storybook rhyme steps from the page. What was it doing to me?"

Vendanj eyed him. Tapped his own chest. "You felt it in here."

Tahn nodded.

"A renderer of the Will can move things," he explained. "Push them. Sometimes you'll see what he does. Sometimes you won't." He took a long breath. "Sometimes it's outside the body. And other times," Vendanj tapped his chest again, "it's in here."

"I don't feel the same," Tahn said.

"It's Resonance." Vendanj said it with obvious concern. "It'll linger like a played note. Won't ever go away completely. But it'll stop feeling like it does today."

Tahn rubbed his chest. "I felt like I was remembering. . . ." But it hadn't completely come back. Mostly the *feeling* of the memory remained. He turned to Vendanj. "What did it mean, 'There'll be no heroes this time'?"

Vendanj took a storyteller's breath. "This plateau used to be part of the flatlands below." He gestured out over the bluff . "The Sedagin people here are known as the Right Arm of the Promise. Masters of the longblade. They've always kept the First Promise; always marched against the Quiet when they come."

"What about this time?" Tahn asked, looking at the dead Velle.

Vendanj didn't seem to hear him. "First time the Quiet came, the regent of Recityv called a Convocation of Seats. Every nation and throne was asked to join an alliance to meet the threat. And most did. The Sedagin were the strongest part of that army. And the Quiet were pushed back.

"Ages later, the Quiet came again." Vendanj shook his head and sighed. "But by then Convocation had become a political game. Kings committed only token regiments. So, the regent Corihehn adjourned Convocation and sent word to Holivagh, leader of the Sedagin, to march toward the Pall mountains. He told him there was a Second Promise from this Second Convocation. He told him an alliance army would meet them there."

Tahn guessed the next part, disgust rising in his throat. "It was a lie."

"It was a lie," Vendanj echoed, nodding. "Twenty thousand Sedagin soldiers cut a path through the Quiet. They reached the Pall mountains where Bourne armies were crossing into the Eastlands, but by then only two thousand Sedagin were left. Still, they held the breach for eight days. They waited for Corihehn's reinforcements. But the army of the Second Promise never came. And every Sedagin bladesman perished."

"But we won the war," Tahn added, tentative.

"When Del'Agio, Randeur of the Sheason, learned what Corihehn had done, he sent Sheason messengers into the courts of every city. They threatened death to any who wouldn't honor Corihehn's lie. The Castigation, it was called."

Vendanj looked up and down the edge of the bluff. "When the war was won, the Sheason came into the high plains. For several cycles of the first moon they linked hands and willed the earth to rise, built an earthen monument to the Sedagin. Gave them a home. These plains are known as Teheale. It means 'earned in blood' in the Covenant Tongue."

Tahn sat silent in reverence to the sacrifice made so long ago.

"Seems our Velle friend doesn't think Sheason and Sedagin can turn the Quiet back again." Vendanj's smile caught in the light of the moon. "No heroes."

In many ways, Vendanj reminded Tahn of his father, Balatin. Serious, but able to let worry go when he sensed Tahn needed to laugh or just let things lie. Tahn suddenly missed his father, a deep missing. His da had gone to his earth a few years ago, leaving Tahn and Wendra to make their way alone—their mother, Vocencia, had died a few years before Balatin. He missed her, too.

"It'll look something like this." Vendanj gestured away from the high plateau again, shifting topics. "The Heights of Restoration, Tahn. On the far side of the Saeculorum."

"Because you think this time *I'm* the hero?" He stared at the steam rising from the dead Bar'dyn's wounds.

Vendanj sighed. "I'm inclined to agree with the Velle. And I don't think like that anymore." He paused, his eyes distant. "If I ever did."

"He said there were others," Tahn pressed. "Called me a mule."

Vendanj gave a dismissive laugh over that. "We're all mules. Each hauling some damn load, don't you think?"

Tahn waited, making clear he wanted an answer. He'd agreed to come. He was bone weary, and scared to think Vendanj had pinned too much hope on him.

Tahn could hit almost anything with his bow. There'd been countless hours of practice supervised by his father. Even before that, he'd had a sure hand.

Somewhere in those lost years of his young life he'd obviously learned its use; fighting techniques, too—his reactions were like Mira's Latae battle forms, just less polished. But against an army? Against Velle? That thing had taken hold of him somehow. Not just his body, but *who* he was. It had stroked painful memories, giving them new life in his mind. It was a pain unlike anything he'd yet felt. This was madness.

What the hell am I doing?

The Sheason seemed to know his thoughts, and put a hand on Tahn's shoulder. "There's a sense about you, Tahn. Like the words you use when you draw your bow." He paused. "But no, you're not the only one we've taken to Restoration. Remember what I said at the start: We believe you can stand there. You've not passed your Change, so the burdens of your mistakes aren't fully on you yet. That'll make it easier."

"Why would you need *me* if you've taken others?"

Vendanj let out a long breath. He settled a gaze on Tahn that spoke of disappointment and regret. "None have survived Tillinghast." He paused as if weighing Tahn's resolve. "That's its old name. Tillinghast is where the Heights of Restoration fall away." He gestured again toward the cliff's edge close by. "Like this bluff."

Before Tahn could comment, Vendanj pushed on. "And that's those who went at all. Most chose not to go. Your willingness. It sets you apart from most."

"He's right," Mira added, approval in her voice.

Tahn looked up at her, finding encouragement in her silver-grey eyes. She showed him the barest of smiles. And warmth flooded his chest and belly, chasing out some of the deep shiver still lingering inside him.

"Tahn," Vendanj said, gathering his attention again. "The thing you need to remember is this. Standing at Tillinghast isn't just about what ever mettle's in you to survive its touch. It's more about whether or not you can suffer the change it'll cause in you once it's done."

Tahn shook his head, panic fluttering anew in his chest. "What change?"

"Different for everyone who stands there," Vendanj replied.

"If they *live*," Tahn observed with sharp sarcasm. "And then do what?"

"If the Quiet fully break free of the Bourne"—Mira nodded as though it was only a matter of time—"they'll come with elder beings. Creatures against which steel is useless."

Vendanj got to his feet. "And my order is at odds with itself. Diminished because of it." He looked down at Tahn. "This time . . . we've asked *you* to go to Tillinghast. The Veil that holds the Quiet at bay is weakening. Could be that the Song of Suffering that keeps it strong is failing. I know there are few with the ability to sing Suffering. But whatever the reason for the Veil's weakness, we think—if you can stand at Tillinghast—you can help should a full Quiet army come."

Tahn shook his head in disbelief. And fear. "All because of the damned words I can't help but say every time I draw." He shook his bow. "And because I have a *sense*. Maybe it's time you restore my memory. Give me back those twelve years you say you took from me when you sent me to the Hollows."

He wanted that more than he let on. His earliest memories began just six years ago. *Twelve years. Gone.* And until Vendanj had come into the Hollows, Than had thought maybe he'd had some sort of accident. Hit his head. Lost his memory. But the Sheason had taken it. To protect him, the man had said.

"You may believe you're ready for that. But think about it." He pointed at the Velle, which had surfaced searing memories in him. "You don't remember your young life . . . but it was a hard one. Not *all* hard. But most of it was spent in an unhappy place. And now, you're far from home, chased by Quiet, asked to climb to Tillinghast, and you're coming soon to the age of accountability."

Tahn had been eager for his Standing and the Change that came after his eighteenth year. Eager for what, he didn't exactly know. To be taken more seriously was part of it, though. And because he'd thought he might somehow get his memory back.

Tahn stood, shouldered his bow. "Wouldn't that suggest I'm old enough—"

"No, it wouldn't," Vendanj cut in sharply. "I took your memory all those years ago as a protection to you. It still is. Before we reach Tillinghast I'll return it to you. You'll need it there." He put his hand again on Tahn's shoulder, his hard expression softening. "But not now. Trust me on this. I've seen what it does to a mind when so much change comes at once."

Tahn thought about the pressure in his body and mind when the Velle had taken hold of him. The things it had surfaced all in a rush. Jagged, ugly things to remember.

Images of young friends, though he couldn't see their faces. A fight, though he couldn't remember why. Except they were settling something. The feeling of betrayal lingered. A sad pain in the pit of his stomach.

Tahn walked to where the Velle lay. Something glinted on the ground near its body. He hunkered down and ran his fingers across a smooth surface glistening with moonlight. Felt like glass. At its center were two fist-sized holes.

"What's this?"

Vendanj came up beside him. "Velle won't bear the cost of rendering the Will. They transfer it. Take the vitality of anything at hand so they can remain strong."

The Velle had thrust its hands into the soil. Darkness had flared. It had caused the formation of this thin crust of dark glass. Tahn stepped on it. A soft *pop*. A fragile sound. If Vendanj hadn't been here, what else inside Tahn would the Velle have taken hold of?

He finally gave a low, resigned laugh. "You win. Why complicate all this fun we're having, right?"

He stole a look at Mira, who showed him her slim smile again. That, at least, was helpful. Hopeful, too. Like the lighter shades of blue strengthening in the east behind her.

Just before he turned away, he caught sight of low fogs gathering on the lowland floor. He pointed. "You see that?"

Vendanj looked, and his expression hardened. Soon Mira stood with them, as they watched a cloud bank form around the base of the plateau.

"Je'holta," Vendanj said.

"What is it?" Tahn asked.

"Another form of Quiet." He paused a long moment. "And something we'll now have to pass through when we leave here."

Mira's smile was gone. "Good test for Tillinghast."

Tahn gave them each a long look, and said without humor, "I just came out to watch the sunrise...."

About the Author

PETER ORULLIAN has worked at Xbox for over a decade, which is good, because he's a gamer. He's toured internationally with various bands and been a featured vocalist at major rock and metal festivals, which is good, because he's a musician.

He's also learned when to hold his tongue, which is good, because he's a contrarian.

Peter has published several short stories, which he thinks are good. *The Unremembered* and *Trial of Intentions* are his first novels, which he hopes you will think are good. He lives in Seattle, where it rains all the damn time. He has nothing to say about that. Visit Peter at: www.orullian.com

Made in the USA
San Bernardino, CA
19 February 2016